"Todd, if yo⎯⎯⎯⎯⎯⎯⎯ ny-more—"

"*No*—that's n⎯⎯⎯⎯⎯⎯ guess I just need a little time. You know, to talk to Gin-Yung—work things out. I still care about her, I guess, but I'm not sure if it's out of obligation or . . ." He trailed off, as if he couldn't bring himself to finish the sentence. "I just don't want to do anything to hurt her."

"Would you rather hurt me again?" Elizabeth asked, almost immediately regretting it.

"No, Liz! It's just that Gin-Yung and I never really broke up—not officially. I'm not sure where we stand. How do *I* know what she thinks?"

"You could ask her." Elizabeth was surprised at the coolness in her own voice.

"I will. I just don't know where to start. And I don't know what I'll do if she—"

"If she's still in love with you?"

"Maybe."

"If she is, Todd, what will you do? Will you go back to her?"

Todd winced, and that one involuntary gesture told Elizabeth everything she didn't want to hear.

Bantam Books in the Sweet Valley University series.
Ask your bookseller for the books you have missed.

And don't miss these Sweet Valley
University Thriller Editions:

SWEET VALLEY UNIVERSITY®

Elizabeth's Heartbreak

Written by
Laurie John

Created by
FRANCINE PASCAL

BANTAM BOOKS
NEW YORK · TORONTO · LONDON · SYDNEY · AUCKLAND

RL 6, age 12 and up

ELIZABETH'S HEARTBREAK
A Bantam Book / March 1997

*Sweet Valley High® and Sweet Valley University®
are registered trademarks of Francine Pascal.
Conceived by Francine Pascal.
Produced by Daniel Weiss Associates, Inc.
33 West 17th Street
New York, NY 10011.*

ISBN: 0-553-57052-8

Published simultaneously in the United States and Canada

*Bantam Books are published by Bantam Books, a division of Bantam
Doubleday Dell Publishing Group, Inc. Its trademark, consisting of the
words "Bantam Books" and the portrayal of a rooster, is Registered in
U.S. Patent and Trademark Office and in other countries. Marca
Registrada. Bantam Books, 1540 Broadway, New York, New York 10036.*

PRINTED IN THE UNITED STATES OF AMERICA

OPM   0 9 8 7 6 5 4 3 2 1

To Elizabeth Bobrick

Chapter One

"You've really outdone yourself this time, Todd. This place is beautiful. Absolutely beautiful."

Elizabeth Wakefield looked up at the old southern plantation facade of Rue Lafayette, her heart fluttering with excitement. It was the most romantic place she'd ever seen. It looked almost too perfect, like a movie set.

As she gently pressed her fingertips against one of the ornate Greek columns, Elizabeth almost expected the whole structure to topple over and fall to the ground. When it held fast, she smiled. *It's real,* she thought. *Everything here is real. I feel like I'm dreaming, but I'm not.*

She smoothed down the hem of her twin sister's pink chiffon baby-doll dress, silently thanking Jessica for letting her borrow it. The satin spaghetti straps bared her shoulders and made her feel slightly self-conscious, but at the same time she felt pretty and elegant—like royalty.

But maybe it wasn't the dress at all. Maybe she felt pretty and elegant simply because she was so happy.

Elizabeth couldn't remember the last time she had been so happy. *And why shouldn't I be?* she thought. Tonight she was back on the arm of her high-school boyfriend and first true love, Todd Wilkins. To celebrate their reunion, he was taking her to an intimate dinner at the exclusive and fashionable restaurant in the Rue Lafayette hotel.

While Todd adjusted his cuff links, Elizabeth took a long, appreciative look at him. In all the years that Elizabeth and Todd had known each other, Todd had never looked better than he did tonight. His dark, tailored suit fit every inch of him perfectly. The cut of his jacket emphasized his strong shoulders and broad chest. Elizabeth couldn't help but let out a sigh.

"This place really *is* unbelievable." Todd whistled as he took in the hotel's main entrance. A fan-shaped window of intricately etched glass was set above two heavy, carved oak doors. The brass doorknobs were shaped like rams' heads. "It's a long way from the Dairi Burger, isn't it?"

Elizabeth laughed brightly. "I guess it'll have to do for tonight."

"I don't know, Liz. Do you think their fries will be as good?"

"Do me a favor, Todd," Elizabeth said, holding up her hands in mock protest. "*Don't* order a burger and fries."

Todd chuckled. "I'm pretty sure that burgers and fries won't be on the menu this evening." Todd grasped a ram's head doorknob and pulled. The door swung open heavily. "After you, *mademoiselle*," he said, giving Elizabeth a quick, tingling kiss as she walked past him.

When Elizabeth crossed over the threshold, she gasped. Stepping inside the Rue Lafayette hotel was like stepping into another era—or another world entirely. The grand lobby cut through the center of the building from top to bottom. Elizabeth was speechless as her eyes traveled upward past each of three balconied floors, finally coming to rest on an enormous, dome shaped skylight. On her right was a private library that had been turned into a rare-book shop. On her left was the check-in area for hotel patrons and a wrought-iron staircase leading up to the rooms in a broad, sweeping spiral.

The gentle pressure of Todd's hand on her bare arm brought her back to ground level. "Come on, Liz," Todd said, his brown eyes dancing. "Let's go celebrate."

"After *you, monsieur,*" Elizabeth responded, holding up her face for another kiss.

Elizabeth's heels clicked loudly on the marble floor as Todd led her back to what would have been the building's salon a century or so ago. The lavishly decorated room now served as the dining area for the restaurant. There was only room enough for fifteen tables.

"Oh, Todd, this is so romantic," Elizabeth breathed, squeezing Todd's arm in anticipation.

"I still can't believe I got a reservation," Todd responded. "But I guess Wednesday nights aren't as busy."

They were greeted by a painfully thin, middle-aged hostess in a long black gown. She asked Todd's name and triple-checked her reservation book.

"Ah, yes, Mr. Wilkins, here you are. Follow me, please." The hostess led them past immaculately dressed couples who sat gracefully at tables laden with fine china and silver. "Will this be suitable?" she asked, coming to a stop next to a table that looked no less exquisite than any of the others.

Todd squared his shoulders and nodded.

"Enjoy."

"Thank you," Todd said as the hostess walked away. He pulled out a hand-carved chair for Elizabeth, but just as she sat down on the emerald green velvet cushion, he snapped his fingers. "Wait—I almost forgot something. Just a sec, Liz. I'll be right back."

Elizabeth was surprised to see Todd dash over to the hostess, exchange a few words, and disappear into the lobby. But most everything that had happened to her lately had been surprising.

After her traumatic breakup with her long-time boyfriend, Tom Watts, Elizabeth had gone to a frat party in an attempt to ease her pain. But instead of finding a good time, she had found a pack of frat brothers who got her drunk and began to harass her.

Todd had stepped in at just the right moment, rescuing Elizabeth when things had started to get out of hand. And that night Todd had kissed her for the first time since the two of them had broken up so many months before. Even though Elizabeth knew deep down that she needed some time alone to heal, she couldn't get Todd out of her mind. And now, after a few false starts and a lot of soul-searching, Elizabeth and Todd were back together and celebrating in style.

She glanced around the luxurious green-and-gold room. The cool darkness created by the deep green carpeted floor was offset by gold-flecked wallpaper and gold-framed mirrors. A glittering crystal chandelier twinkled in the center of the high ceiling, and candles on each table

gave everything a romantic glow. The entire ·
scene seemed to be right out of *Gone with the
Wind*. Elizabeth could just see Scarlett O'Hara
ripping the thick velvet drapes from the windows to turn into a makeshift gown.

A server arrived with a bottle of spring water
and two crystal goblets. As he prepared the
water Elizabeth anxiously tugged at a long
blond curl that had escaped from her updo.
What could be taking Todd so long?

Elizabeth thanked the server as he handed
her a small, hand-lettered menu on creamy
paper. She picked up her water goblet and
dropped it right back down on the table when
she got a good look at the menu. *Everything is
so expensive!* Elizabeth thought, alarmed.

She hastily began blotting spilled drops of
water off the menu with her linen napkin. The
drops were threatening to blur the hand-written
menu completely. *Maybe if I can creatively smear
the prices, the dinner won't cost so much,* she
imagined, her heart pounding.

"Wipe that look off your face, Elizabeth
Wakefield. I could read your mind from across
the room."

"Todd!" Elizabeth gasped, looking up at his
sweetly concerned face. "If I'd known this place
was so pricey—"

"It's OK, Liz," Todd said, grinning and

shaking his head as if he had expected to have this conversation. "Don't you worry about a thing tonight. Believe me, I can handle it."

"But—"

"No buts," Todd demanded, taking his seat across from her. "I've been saving up for a night like this. Now that we're back together again, I can't think of a better way to spend my money."

Elizabeth blushed. "Todd, you didn't have to—"

"Yes, I did." Todd smiled gently and produced a single, perfect long-stemmed red rose from underneath his jacket and held it over the table. "For you," he whispered.

As Elizabeth reached up to take the rose from Todd's hand, a tingle went up her spine. She could feel tears of joy coming to her eyes. "It's beautiful. The rose, this place . . . everything. Thank you."

"No, thank *you*. Thank you for giving me another chance. You don't know how much that means to me, Liz."

Elizabeth cast her eyes downward and looked at the rose. She stroked the petals gently. "I think I do know," she said quietly.

Just then the server returned to their table and began reading off the specials for the evening. Elizabeth only half listened, relieved that she had a moment to gather her thoughts and emotions. Her head was spinning too quickly; she was dizzy with contentment.

Suddenly Todd cleared his throat. "Liz, have you decided yet?"

"Um . . ." Elizabeth quickly looked back over her smeared menu. "I'll have the shrimp Creole. And a salad."

"Two salads to start," Todd told the server confidently. "Shrimp Creole for the lady. And I'll have the filet mignon."

"Excellent," the server said, picking up the menus and walking away briskly. Elizabeth was relieved that the server didn't seem to notice that she'd ruined hers.

Todd turned to Elizabeth, his eyes warm. "I hope we'll have room for dessert after all that. I hear their pecan and sweet potato pies are out of this world."

"I don't think that'll be a problem for you, Todd," Elizabeth said with a giggle. "You could probably have three orders of filet mignon and still be hungry for more."

"We'll see about that," Todd replied, taking a sip of his water. "The servings here are supposed to be gigantic."

The server returned with a fresh bottle of spring water and two of the biggest, greenest, most tempting-looking salads Elizabeth had ever seen.

Todd took a bite and groaned softly. He pointed his salad fork toward his plate and nodded. "You know, I think this may be the first time I've ever tasted lettuce. I mean *really* tasted it. I can never go back to that pale, shredded junk in the cafeteria again."

Elizabeth dug into her salad. Todd was right—it *was* delicious and fresh. And when their main courses arrived, Elizabeth couldn't believe her eyes. The portions were huge and artfully arranged.

"How did you find out about this place, Todd?" Elizabeth asked as she cut a huge Creole shrimp in half.

Todd looked at her hesitantly. "Do you really want to know?"

Elizabeth's forehead creased. "Why do you ask?"

"I saw a review of it on WSVU."

The mention of the college television station where Elizabeth and Tom Watts had worked together made her cringe slightly, but she shrugged it off. "That's OK."

"Sorry, Liz. I didn't want to bring up anything—"

"No, really," Elizabeth interrupted him. "It's OK."

"So . . . ," Todd began shyly. "At the risk of spoiling a perfect evening, I have to know. Are you over him? Tom, I mean?"

Elizabeth put down her fork and forced herself to remember how badly Tom Watts had hurt her. She had gone to him for comfort and support after Tom's own father, George Conroy, had made a pass at her. Instead of believing Elizabeth, Tom had broken up with her, accusing her of making up the whole story. And last week, after Tom had taunted Elizabeth in the middle of the quad and called her a liar, she had spotted him out on a date with a woman she'd never seen before, looking totally happy and guilt-free.

As she looked across the table at Todd's openly loving face glowing in the candlelight, there was no longer any question in her mind about how she felt about Tom Watts. "Yes, Todd," Elizabeth said assuredly. "I'm over him. Completely."

Todd let out a sigh of what appeared to be pure relief. "I'm glad to hear that. Really. I'm not going to ask you if you're sure, because you sound sure."

"I am," Elizabeth replied, hesitating to pick her fork back up again. A question hovered on the tip of her tongue—a question she dreaded asking. But she and Todd were so close and had known each other for so long, Elizabeth knew there was nothing she couldn't ask him.

"Todd," she began, "as long as we're on the subject, I have to know. What about you and Gin-Yung?"

"Well, you know that when she left for her internship in London, we had decided that it was OK to see other people while she was away."

"I know. But . . . have you talked to her lately? Does she know about us?"

Todd paused thoughtfully. "I talked to her a few times last week, but it was strange. We really didn't have anything to say to each other. I think we've totally drifted apart."

"But have you told her about us?"

"I haven't heard from her since you and I got back together," Todd answered straightforwardly. "I'll tell her, Elizabeth. The first chance I get."

Elizabeth played with her fork, afraid of how Todd might answer her final question. "Do you still love her?"

Todd finished his last bite of filet mignon, slowly wiped his mouth, and dropped the linen napkin beside his plate. "I don't know if I was ever really in love with Gin-Yung. I mean, I care about her, and she could always make me laugh. She was a great friend, but I'm not sure I ever loved her. At least, not the way I love you." Todd reached across the table and took Elizabeth's hand in his. "And I do love you, Elizabeth. So much."

Elizabeth felt a charge go up her arm and through her body as Todd squeezed her hand.

"I love you too, Todd," she said, reeling from the intensity in his brown eyes as they shone in the flickering candlelight.

Gin-Yung Suh sat propped amid a pile of pillows in her father's recliner, still exhausted from jet lag. Even though her flight to Sweet Valley from London had been five whole days ago, she just couldn't regain her strength.

Program after program flickered across the television screen in front of her as she idly pressed the channel button on the remote. She rarely let any single station stay on the screen for more than ten seconds.

She paused slightly longer on ESPN. But even a good soccer match couldn't hold her interest tonight. Her enthusiasm for soccer—and all sports in general—had waned away to practically nothing.

Just a few months ago, I was determined to become the greatest sports reporter who ever lived, Gin-Yung thought. *Now it all seems like a stupid, childish fantasy.*

Sports didn't matter anymore. Journalism didn't matter anymore. Nothing seemed to matter to Gin-Yung—except, possibly, Todd Wilkins.

Yes, Todd does matter, Gin-Yung realized. *I wish he was here with me right now.* She wanted to feel his strong arms around her, to absorb the energy and courage she so desperately needed. Her chest ached whenever she thought about him. *But what's one more ache, more or less? If I can cope with this throbbing headache, I can cope with a small case of heartache.*

But even though Gin-Yung knew she wanted to see him, she wasn't all that certain that Todd wanted to see her. Their last few phone calls had turned out to be horribly distant and awkward. Todd had said nothing personal, nothing that let her know that he was missing her. There had been more minutes of dead air than there'd been of conversation.

Perhaps that was Gin-Yung's own fault too. She couldn't think of much to say herself. Gin-Yung had been feeling so depressed that she couldn't muster up the energy to make small talk. Nothing seemed important enough to bring up, except for the very thing she was too scared to tell him.

Wouldn't it be ironic if Todd thinks my *feelings for* him *have cooled down!* she thought. That would certainly explain his awkwardness on the phone. But the first chance Gin-Yung got, she would let him know that she still cared about him. Todd would understand.

But would he understand the reason she came back to Sweet Valley? If she told him everything now, how would he react? How could she expect him to understand when she didn't understand herself?

Gin-Yung massaged her temples with one hand. All these thoughts were just giving her a headache. When her mother and older sister, Kim-Mi, came into the room, she dropped the remote and folded both her hands in her lap.

"What are you doing up, darling?" her mother asked. She was wearing the same mask of concern that she'd worn ever since meeting Gin-Yung at the airport last Friday night. "You should be in bed."

"Lying in bed isn't going to help me, Mother."

The wrinkles on her mother's face deepened. "You should get plenty of rest. You should—"

"I'm tired of lying in bed. I feel like I'm just wasting my time."

Kim snatched up the remote and pressed the mute button. "And I suppose watching old re-runs of *Bewitched* is more productive," she said sarcastically.

Gin-Yung could always count on her big sister to be straightforward and speak her mind, but tonight Gin-Yung wasn't in the mood for Kim's frankness.

"What exactly do you suggest I do, Kim?" Gin-Yung asked tartly.

"If I'd just gotten home from abroad, the very first thing I'd do would be to call my boyfriend."

"Well, I'm not you," Gin-Yung snapped, venting some of the anger that had been building up inside her.

Kim didn't seem to take offense. "You should call Todd and ask him to come over. Or better yet, brush your hair, get yourself dressed, and go over to his dorm. Surprise him."

"No!" Gin-Yung gasped. She didn't dare admit to her sister that that was exactly what she'd been wanting to do ever since she'd stepped off the plane. She started to shake her head, but the sudden movement caused the room to spin. Putting a hand to her forehead, she said, "I'm not feeling up to that yet."

Her mother quickly agreed. "That's right. Seeing friends would be much too stressful for you right now, Gin-Yung."

"Todd isn't *just* a friend," Kim pointed out. "He's her *boyfriend,* Mother. What could possibly be stressful about seeing her own boyfriend?"

The stressful part wouldn't be seeing him, Gin-Yung thought. *No, the stressful part will be telling him my secret, and I'm not ready to do that yet.* Even though Gin-Yung was desperate to see Todd, she knew she couldn't face him until she knew *exactly* what she was going to say.

15

Mrs. Suh held up her hand. "Gin-Yung, you should go to your room and rest right now. I'll bring you some hot tea."

"Mother, please stop fussing over me. I'm fine. Just a little tired. Maybe Kim is right. Seeing friends would be good for me. I'll go see Todd . . . tomorrow."

"Very well. But for now, hot tea will help you relax," her mother said. "I'll bring it to your room."

"No, Mother. I'm not going to lie down right now," Gin-Yung replied, suddenly feeling motivated. "In fact, I'm heading outside. I heard on the news that there's going to be a meteor shower tonight. You wanna come watch with me, Kim?"

"Shooting stars? Cool!" Kim said.

"No! Shooting stars are bad luck." Mrs. Suh held out both her arms pleadingly, palms upward.

After seeing the fear on her mother's face, Gin-Yung softened her tone. "That's just an old superstition, Mother."

"Right," Kim agreed. "What's wrong with watching a few hunks of space junk burn up in the atmosphere?"

Mrs. Suh didn't look convinced, but she seemed to back down.

"Are you coming?" Gin-Yung asked Kim again.

"Sure. I'm up for it."

Gin-Yung stumbled slightly as she climbed out of the recliner. Her mother stepped forward to steady her.

"Maybe you could bring the tea outside later, Mother," Gin-Yung said, smiling gratefully.

Mrs. Suh nodded and without a word walked into the kitchen.

"I'll go get the lawn chairs from the garage," Kim said. "Grab a couple of pillows, Gin, and we'll get comfy while we watch the stars fall."

And I'll watch my world collapse, Gin-Yung thought, grabbing up an armload of pillows. *This could be my last chance to see a shooting star.* She picked up the remote and turned off the TV. *My last chance to watch television. My last chance to do anything. Will I have a last chance to be kissed?* She glanced over at the picture of her and Todd Wilkins that sat on the end table and sighed. *I hope so.* She decided right then and there that she couldn't wait around any longer. She would definitely go see Todd tomorrow and tell him everything.

If there is a tomorrow, she thought with a chill as she headed out to join her sister in the backyard.

Tom Watts watched from his car as Dana Upshaw hurried across her tiny, unkempt yard in

17

front of the off-campus house she rented with three other women. He couldn't help but grin at the way she was dressed. The outrageously skimpy purple dress covered with big yellow flowers was plenty wild, but combined with brick red, knee-high boots and a wide-brimmed hat—well, Dana was the artsy type, all right. Tom found it hard to believe that his little half sister's cello teacher could be so *un*–mild mannered.

"So," Tom said as Dana climbed into his car and flounced a bit to adjust her short dress. "Our second date."

She smiled brightly, and he smiled back, hoping she didn't notice how nervous he was. All the way over in the car he'd wondered if he was doing the right thing by asking Dana out again. While they'd had a great time together last Friday at the poetry reading, Tom still hadn't been able to shake the feeling that he might have been forcing himself to have a good time.

At the end of their date, when Tom had dropped Dana off, he couldn't bring himself to give her a good-night kiss—not even a tiny one. Her look of disappointment at that moment had filled him with immense guilt, so he decided to give Dana another chance.

And now that Dana was actually sitting beside him and he could smell her tangy, citrusy perfume, Tom wondered why he could have been so dense. Dana was bright, funny, and talented—not to mention drop-dead gorgeous. Anyone in their right mind could see that Dana was a keeper.

Still, she's no Elizabeth Wake— Tom broke off his thought angrily. *That* was the problem. He couldn't stop comparing Dana to that *other* girl he used to date—the one who'd betrayed him and broken his heart. It wasn't fair—to him *or* to Dana. Why should he let Elizabeth Wakefield continue to make his life miserable?

Well, no more, he thought. New Year's Eve was a long way away, but Tom decided to make a resolution on the spot. *As of right now, I'm never going to think about her again. She no longer exists. Even her name is taboo. I won't say it—I won't even think it.* That old girlfriend clearly didn't care about him, and he didn't care about her—not anymore. The sooner he faced it, the better.

It's time you got on with your life, Watts, Tom told himself. *Quit thinking about your former Ms. Right and concentrate on Ms. Right-here-and-right-now. And now that your brain is on the right track, all you have to do is wait for your heart to catch up with it.* That last thought made him groan internally.

Tom's train of thought was broken by a slender hand waving a slip of paper in front of his face. "Hello . . . Earth to Tom."

19

"Wha—oh, sorry, Dana, I was just . . . remembering something I forgot to take care of at WSVU."

"It's OK, Tom," Dana replied, her smile gentle and understanding. "I was just wondering, do you want this ticket or not?" She ran her fingertips along the edge of the ticket playfully.

"What's it for?"

"My big recital tomorrow night. If you can make it."

Tom smiled, happy that she seemed to accept his lame excuse about WSVU. "Sure, Dana. I'd love to. I'm flattered you've invited me."

"Great!" Dana reached over, tucked the ticket into his shirt pocket, and patted his chest. Her hand lingered for a moment longer than necessary, making Tom's mind wander off in yet another direction. Dana's hazel eyes, surrounded by incredibly thick dark lashes, were almost hypnotizing.

"Hey, wake up. I'm still here." Dana tapped the end of Tom's nose with the tip of her finger. "What's on the agenda for tonight? I hope I dressed appropriately."

"You look great, Dana." He helped her snap her seat belt into place. "Actually, um, the agenda's pretty open for tonight. I didn't have anything definite planned." Of course, Tom didn't want to admit that the real reason he had no plans was that every time he'd come up with an idea, it would remind him of Eliz—that *other* girl. "What are you up for?"

"Well, we aren't going to just sit here in my driveway all night, are we?" Dana teased. "If we are, maybe we should get a little more comfortable."

He grinned. "No, of course not. Tonight we'll do whatever *you* want. It's your choice—just name it."

"Let's start with just driving around," she suggested. "We don't have to do anything special. Just being with you is enough for me." She reached over and caressed his arm.

Tom started the car. But as he pulled away from the curb he couldn't help thinking, *I wish it was enough for me too.*

The orange Volkswagen Beetle lurched forward and coughed as Winston Egbert shoved the stick into park and turned off the ignition. Ahead of him the grassy hillside next to the science building was dotted with coolers, blankets, lawn chairs, and students.

"Don't bump that car with your door," Winston warned his girlfriend, Denise Waters, as he pointed toward the gold Mercedes in the parking space next to the passenger side.

"Why, Winnie? Are you afraid I'll scratch its paint and you'll have to fight its owner to defend my honor?" Denise cracked as she jumped out of the Beetle.

"No, I'm afraid you'll scratch *my* car's paint," Winston replied sarcastically. "Then I'll have to fight *you* to defend *its* honor." He got out of the car and ran around to meet his girlfriend, who was admiring the gold Mercedes. "Good thing the science building has an equal-opportunity parking lot," Winston kidded, "otherwise my old pumpkin might get an inferiority complex."

Denise let out a low whistle. "Nice car, but it looks a little out of place here. What student could afford a machine like that?"

"Duh?" Winston rolled his eyes. "Try Lila Fowler, Bruce Patman, Alison Quinn . . ." Winston began counting off their rich classmates on his fingers.

"OK, OK, I get your drift," Denise said, linking her arm with his. They squeezed carefully past the Mercedes and started up the hill.

"Can you believe this crowd?" Denise said. "It looks like a carnival out here."

"Hey, bonus points are bonus points," Winston replied. "Professor Hodges made the same deal in all her classes. Anyone who shows up to watch the meteor shower gets twenty-five of them. And believe me, points are not usually this easy to come by in her classes."

"So I've heard. Twenty-five points will just about bring your grade up to a B, won't it?"

"Very funny. I'll have you know I'm pulling a B-plus right now in astronomy. I could very well be on my way to an A with these extra points."

"Winnie, you're *always* on your way to an A. Whether you get there or not remains to be seen."

"It could happen," Winston joked.

Denise shook her head. "Hey, look, isn't that Nina and Bryan?" she asked, pointing to a couple busily assembling a telescope.

"Yeah, like they *really* need bonus points."

"Maybe they're out here for their own edification."

"Oooh, *edification.* I'm so proud to have a girlfriend who still remembers her SAT words!"

Denise playfully slugged Winston's arm. "You'd better go sign in, Einstein. I know you can use all the bonus points you can get."

Winston worked his way through the crowd as Denise started spreading a plaid stadium blanket on the grassy hillside.

"Maybe we should have brought a picnic," Winston said when he returned to their spot. He lay down on the blanket and started to trace designs on Denise's arm.

Denise didn't seem to get the hint. "There's Alex and Noah. It looks like they have a pizza. Want to join them?" she asked, waving to a nearby couple who were seated in lawn chairs.

"Hey, are we here to eat, socialize, or make out?" Winston kidded, running his hand up Denise's silky leg.

"What?" Denise said with mock indignation. "I thought we came out here to watch shooting stars."

"No, we came out here to get bonus points. I'll get them whether I see twinkling stars, shooting stars, movie stars, or just the stars in your eyes, my darling." Winston puckered up his lips for a big smooch.

"You're incorrigible!" Denise laughed and pushed her hand in his face.

Winston kissed it anyway. "You love me in spite of it."

"No, Winnie," Denise said as she lay back and nuzzled against his shoulder. "I love you *because* of it."

"There's one!" someone shouted. "There's a shooting star!"

Heads turned as a glittering gold speck streaked across the black sky. A temporary hush fell across the crowd, followed by some "ooohs" and "aaahs" as a larger meteor blazed overhead.

Some students watched the sky intently. Others returned to heavenly bodies nearer at hand and wouldn't have noticed a meteor if it had crashed at their feet. No one, including Winston and Denise, paid much attention to the well-dressed, middle-aged, slightly balding man who sat alone on a rock with his binoculars trained—not on the sky—but on the parking area behind Dickenson Hall, where a happy young couple was kissing good night.

Chapter
Two

". . . and that's why Nick Fox is the best boyfriend in the world," Jessica Wakefield announced to a standing-room-only crowd. The lounge of the Theta Alpha Theta sorority house was packed with women who were waiting for their vice president, Alison Quinn, to show up at the special Thursday morning meeting she'd called.

Jessica sat on the faded Victorian sofa in front of a scarred cherry coffee table where Isabella Ricci had spread bottles of polish, emery boards, and other manicure paraphernalia. With Isabella in the sorority, none of the Thetas had an excuse for having nails that were anything less than perfect.

With an elegantly bored expression Lila Fowler, Jessica's best friend, sat on a large pillow beside the coffee table while Isabella finished painting her nails Violent Violet.

"What time did Alison say to be here?" Lila asked.

"Twelve-fifteen," Isabella answered. "And as usual, she's the last to show."

"She *always* does this!" Jessica complained. "I guess she thinks none of us have lives."

Jessica had tried in the past to get along with Alison Quinn—in the spirit of Theta sisterhood, of course. But even that pretense was long gone now. Jessica couldn't stand Alison, and there was no doubt in her mind that Alison felt the same way about her.

"Thanks for the manicure, Izzy," Lila said, settling herself onto the sofa. She held up her hand to compare her nail color to her shimmering, deep purple silk blouse. The match was perfect. Gracefully Lila put her hands out in front of her and sat with such poise and finesse that one would never guess she was simply waiting for her polish to dry. In fact, she looked as if she were posing for the cover of a French fashion magazine. And for Lila Fowler that was never much of a stretch.

"Do mine next," Jessica insisted, slipping into the spot that Lila had just vacated. "Use that peach color. It's a perfect match for the new sundress I bought last weekend. I can't wait for Nick to see me in it."

27

"Oh no," Denise Waters said, laying down her history book. "I believe I feel another Nick Fox story coming on."

Everyone around them either groaned or giggled.

"You guys can laugh," Jessica said indignantly, "but until you're really in love, you don't know what it's like."

"I don't know why we wouldn't," Isabella said, her gray eyes twinkling as she gently shook the bottle of peach polish. "We've already heard how perfect Nick is at least fifteen times today. 'Nick Fox is so mature and adventurous.' 'Nick Fox is the sexiest man alive.' 'Nick has the most absolutely perfect, make-you-melt, jade green eyes.'" Isabella put her hand to her forehead in an exaggerated pantomime of a swooning southern belle.

"And 'he's got a low, husky voice that simply makes my knees weak,'" Lila whispered hoarsely.

"And a totally pumped physique—you know, 'muscles that Superman would kill for,'" Isabella continued.

"I heard he has dimples that could be registered as lethal weapons," Denise Waters added. She poked her own cheeks to create mock dimples.

"Did anyone mention that he looks like a Levi's jeans model . . . from the back?" Alexandra Rollins offered.

"Oooh, listen to you, Alex!" Denise teased.

"Don't look at me. I'm just quoting Jessica."

They're sooo *jealous,* Jessica thought with a proud smile. "Well, don't forget about him being the world's best kisser."

"How would we know that his kisses are so great?" Lila asked. "Maybe we should all march down to the police station and put the famous detective's lips to the test." She blew on her nails with a flourish as all the Thetas giggled.

"Don't even think about it," Jessica squealed, teasingly throwing a frayed Victorian pillow in Lila's direction. She knew Lila would never make a move on Nick. Lila was dating Bruce Patman, whom they'd both known since grade school. Bruce was just about as rich as Lila was, so naturally they made the perfect couple.

"Hold still, Jess, before you end up with peach-colored knuckles," Isabella warned, waving the nail-polish brush threateningly.

"Well, you all can laugh, but someday when you meet the perfect man, you'll know why I talk about him so much."

Jessica climbed onto the sofa beside Lila and began to blow on her nail polish.

"What time is it now?" Lila asked, stifling a bored yawn. "I don't have time to sit around here all day. As entertaining as Jess's love life is, I have my own to take care of. I'm supposed to meet Bruce in the coffee shop at one."

"And some of us have studying to do," Denise said, giving her heavy history book a decisive pat.

There were a few boos and moans.

"Speak for yourself, Denise," Mandy Carmichael shouted. Although Theta Alpha Theta was the most popular and prestigious sorority on campus, studying wasn't usually high on their priority list.

"Well, if Her Majesty Queen Alison doesn't show up in ten more minutes, I'm leaving," Lila said.

"I think Alison only calls these meetings to get attention anyway," Alex said, pulling back the rich satin drapes. "What's this 'important meeting' supposed to be about?"

"Who knows? I'm getting to where I cringe every time Alison calls us together," Isabella said.

"Whoa," Jessica said. "You don't think Celine is out of jail, do you?"

Alison's last few 'important meetings' had been for the purpose of shoving the Hell's Belle—Miss Celine Boudreaux of the Louisiana Boudreaux—down their throats. With the promise of a newly redecorated lounge, Alison had succeeded in cajoling the majority of members into making Celine a Theta. But now it was

Celine's fault they were sitting on their shabby old furniture again.

As it turned out, Celine's generous donation turned out to be on empty credit cards. She had originally intended to pay for the renovation with the money she'd hoped to make from a cocaine deal she had been masterminding. But Jessica had stumbled into it, totally by accident, and was the one who got arrested. Celine was willing to let Jessica take the blame, but after the deal fell through, Celine was left without any cash for her creditors—or for her supplier. In the end Celine was rightfully arrested, Jessica was cleared of the charges, and all the Thetas' lovely new furniture had been repossessed.

Luckily their old furniture hadn't been disposed of yet. Now it would be ages before they could afford to replace it. They practically had to use up their whole treasury just to pay for the carpets, wallpaper, and drapes. Pierre's Interiors couldn't very well scrape the paper off the walls and peel up the carpeting to sell to another customer!

"I'm sure Celine won't be free for a long, long time," Lila said.

"I hope Alison's locked up with her," Jessica offered. "Maybe that's why she's so late."

"Uh-oh, reality check," Isabella said just as Alison entered the lounge with Kimberly Schyler and Tina Chai in tow.

"Well, speak of the devil, here come the Three Musketeers now," Alex muttered.

"Looks more like the Three Stooges to me," Jessica whispered.

Immediately Alison took control of the room. "All right, everybody, listen up," she said, clapping three fingers of her right hand against her left palm. "I have important news."

Isabella ignored Alison and motioned Alex over to the coffee table for a manicure. Alex held up her stubby, chewed-on nails and shook her head sadly, but Isabella wouldn't give up.

"*Excuuuse* me," Alison said loudly. "I'm trying to hold a meeting here." She prissed over to the coffee table and tossed her overdone blond hair. "Isabella's Nail Shop is now officially closed. Any other customers will have to wait until the meeting is over. I think you might all want to hear what I have to say today."

Isabella screwed the lid back onto a bottle of Passionate Pink and noisily began tossing her manicure items into her bright green cosmetics case.

"You have our undivided attention, Alison," Jessica said. "Let's hear the big news."

Alison twisted her mouth into a sneer. "Now, I know you've all heard of Bobby Hornet."

"Ooooh, heard him *and* seen him," one of the new pledges squealed.

Everyone giggled.

"Well, he's coming to Sweet Valley this Friday," Alison continued.

The room buzzed with excited whispers.

Alison clapped for attention again. "I know it's not every day that a famous musician stops by, but this is more than simply a personal appearance to sell CDs. There's a special reason for his visit."

For once Jessica was interested in what Alison had to say. Jessica was always interested in a chance to meet celebrities, and Bobby Hornet was one of her favorite singers.

"Bobby Hornet will be choosing models to appear with him in a calendar to raise money for the homeless. It'll be a big seller because it's going to be a totally hot bikini calendar."

"Bobby Hornet in a bikini!" Denise blurted.

"Of *course* Bobby Hornet *won't* be wearing a bikini!" Alison said indignantly. "The girls will. Twelve organizations on campus have been selected to represent SVU on the calendar. Naturally Theta Alpha Theta is one of the twelve. It'll be great publicity for us."

As her audience grew more attentive Alison beamed. "They're going to choose one Theta to represent the sorority. I volunteered, of course. I didn't think anyone else would really want to do it on such short notice. But to be perfectly fair, if anyone else is interested, I can submit your name."

Alison glared around the room as if she wanted to discourage any competition, but it didn't work.

"I'd like to do it," Tina Chai said.

That came as a big surprise to Jessica since Tina was Alison's shadow. Tina rarely smiled unless Alison told her she had something to be happy about.

A pledge raised her hand like she was a first grader asking permission to go to the bathroom.

"Yes, Clarissa?" Alison said.

"Can pledges volunteer?"

"No. I think only a full-fledged Theta should represent us," Alison replied in her best schoolteacher voice. "And it should be someone who holds a responsible position in the sorority. Someone who maintains a decent GPA, not just someone with a good body—although looks should be a very important consideration too, since that's what will sell the calendars."

"Did you hear me volunteer, Alison?" Tina repeated. "I said I'd like to do it."

"Yes, Tina, I got that idea."

"Oooh," Denise whispered under her breath as she and Jessica tried desperately to stifle their giggles.

"I wanna be in it," Mandy Carmichael piped up.

"Me too," said Kimberly Schyler. "I have a new silver lamé bikini, and I've been working on my tan for weeks."

Jessica could practically see Alison's blood pressure rising. Now was the time to put icing on the cake.

"Put my name down too, Alison," Jessica said matter-of-factly, and the entire room went silent.

Immediately Alison seemed to snap. Jessica knew that Alison couldn't stand the idea of having to compete against her.

"Some of you might want to consider the fact that a camera adds ten pounds," Alison replied in a motherly, for-your-own-good voice while glaring right at Jessica.

"It'd take more than ten pounds to flesh out Alison's walking-stick body," Denise whispered to a score of giggles.

"I think Jessica would be a perfect choice," Lila offered.

"Yeah. I move that we take a vote on it," Isabella said.

"Well, that may sound fair, but it won't work." Alison glared at Lila, Isabella, and Jessica, her chin stuck forward, her hands on hips. "You see, Bobby Hornet himself has the final say on who will be in the calendar."

"Well, then, there's no problem. How could

he not want Jessica? Look at her. She's the perfect California girl," Lila said, standing up for her best friend.

Alison's face turned a glorious shade of magenta. "Puh-leeze! That blond-haired, blue-eyed, surfer-girl ideal is simply an outdated stereotype. I'm just as much a California girl as Jessica is. I've lived here all my life." Alison snorted.

"Yes, but you're a little bit hippy for a bikini, aren't you, Alison?" Isabella said snidely.

"I am not hippy! I'll have you know I only wear a size—"

"That was a joke, Alison," Isabella interrupted. "No one would know you had hips if you didn't wear a belt," she added in a whisper, making Jessica sputter with laughter.

Alison steamed. "Very well, I can see you *aren't* going to take this seriously." She slammed a sheet of paper onto the tabletop. "Anyone wanting to volunteer for the calendar spot, sign this sheet. And you might want to gather up a few photos that show how photogenic you are. Bobby Hornet will be screening possible models at Disc-Oh! Music tomorrow afternoon. As I said, the selection is completely up to him. We'll just have to wait until Monday to find out who he chooses."

Jessica leaned back against the lumpy couch

cushions and smiled. *I have it in the bag,* she thought. *Who would possibly choose scrawny Alison Quinn with me in the running? This could be my big break. This calendar shoot could be the beginning of my modeling career.*

Jessica's mind wandered, letting her fantasies develop even further. *Before long I'll be in fashion shows, then on magazine covers, then who knows—I might even get to host "Fashion Château" on the music channel!*

Suddenly a thought brought her free-flying fantasies to a screeching halt. *Nick.* How would Nick feel about seeing his girlfriend hanging on every wall in California, dressed only in a skimpy bikini? And would he even allow her to pose with sexy Bobby Hornet in the first place?

Thursdays were always hectic for Elizabeth. Thanks to a scheduling computer glitch, she had been saddled with back-to-back classes from eight in the morning until one-thirty in the afternoon. By two o'clock she was usually wiped out. But on this particular Thursday, as she and her best friend, Nina Harper, walked across campus from the psychology building, Elizabeth was still on an emotional high from last night's dinner date with Todd. Unconsciously she began to hum a familiar song that had been popular when she was in high school.

"So the date last night went well, did it?" Nina asked, picking up on Elizabeth's cue.

"Excellent," Elizabeth said. "I've hardly been able to pay attention in class all day, just remembering his good-night kiss."

"Mmmm, do tell."

"I don't know if I should. I don't think you're mature enough."

"You're crazy." Nina laughed. "I thought that I looked older and more sophisticated once I lost the beads and braids." Nina ran her hand over her black curls.

"That's true. But I'm talking *major* kiss."

"So let's hear the juicy details."

"You know I'd never kiss and tell."

"*Right.* You know you tell me *everything,* Liz."

Elizabeth laughed. "Aren't you tired of hearing me go on and on about Todd?"

"OK, I know I was a little unsure about you and Todd at first, but you've convinced me—I was wrong. Now, let's have the story. You can't keep going around with that Cheshire Cat grin on your face and not tell me a thing. When are you two going out again?"

"Um, I don't know—tonight, tomorrow night, Saturday, Sunday. Any night he asks."

"Hey, don't get carried away," Nina said, narrowing her dark brown eyes. "You still have to stay on the dean's list."

"Nina, you already study enough for both of us." Nina was a straight-A student—the driven kind. Success was her middle name. Nina was the only person Elizabeth knew who studied more than she did.

Nina switched her heavy stack of books to her other arm. "You're as bad a studyholic as I am, and you know it. You couldn't stand to go out on dates that many nights in a row. You'd have library *withdrawal*."

Elizabeth rolled her eyes. "Nice pun, Nina."

"Well, I'm serious. I give it a week and you'll be telling poor Todd, 'Oh, sorry, sweetie, I can't go out tonight; I have a date with William Shakespeare in the library.'"

"Don't you think he's too old for me?"

The two girls laughed, but Elizabeth knew Nina was probably right.

"Well, at least give me a week to float around on cloud nine before you turn me back into a library pumpkin," Elizabeth said.

"You're mixing metaphors," Nina said with a giggle. "But seriously, Liz, I'm glad things are looking up. It's great seeing you smile again. I know you've had it tough getting over Tom."

"How's Bryan?" Elizabeth asked, quickly changing the subject. She didn't want to be reminded of Tom Watts. Not when her love life was going so smoothly.

"Bryan is busy, as usual. I think he's over at the Black Student Union right now, trying to organize the next March Against Racism. I'm beginning to think he just masquerades as a student to justify his full-time job as BSU president. You know how it is: He does his thing, and I do mine."

"Don't you ever get jealous that he spends so much time away from you?"

"Sometimes, I guess. But deep inside I know I couldn't stand a guy who hovered over me."

"Have you two had a chance to spend any time together at all this week?"

"Oh, sure. In fact, last night we were out watching shooting stars."

Elizabeth's grin dimpled her cheek. "When Jess and I were in junior high, our brother, Steven, and his high-school friends used to say they'd been out watching shooting stars when what they really meant is that they'd been making out with their girlfriends. But why do I get the feeling you were *literally* watching shooting stars?"

"Because that's what we did. We took my telescope over to that hillside by the science building and watched the meteor shower."

"That sounds more like a homework assignment than a date."

Nina laughed. "A date can be wherever you find it!"

"So you two sat around with your eyes glued to a telescope watching for meteors. Knowing you, you probably spent the whole night charting the path and velocity of each one you saw."

"You're just jealous because you were stuck inside some ritzy restaurant with your high-school sweetheart."

"So we're back to that, are we?" Elizabeth raised an eyebrow.

"Yes, and I'm still waiting for details."

"OK, but first finish telling me about the romantic meteor shower."

"It was fun, really. Of course I had to stay up until two this morning studying to make up for the time I missed, but seriously, you and Todd should have seen it. . . ."

Nina's voice trailed off into outer space as Elizabeth happened to notice two girls, their backs to her, sitting on a bench on the quad. One of them had long straight hair; the other had hers cut in a chin-length bob. But their hair was the exact same color—black hair that shone almost blue in the sunlight, just like Gin-Yung Suh's did.

Elizabeth stumbled to a halt as she stared at the girl with the shorter hair. *Gin-Yung? No, it can't be!* she thought feverishly. *My mind must be playing tricks on me. Gin-Yung is in London. Besides, lots of girls have hair like that.* Elizabeth struggled to think of one, but her mind was blazing too quickly.

"C'mon, Liz," Nina called good-naturedly, bringing Elizabeth back to earth. "Quit dreaming. At this rate we'll never make it back to the dorm."

"Uh . . . I just remembered something," Elizabeth said quickly. "I've got to go by WSVU and pick up some notes."

"Want me to come with you?"

"No, I'll be OK."

"You don't look OK." Nina's brow was creased with concern. "In fact, you look terrified. I don't mind coming along in case you run into—"

"No, really, Nina. I'll be fine."

"Well, if you're sure." Nina's look was questioning.

"I'm sure. You go on. I'll catch you back at the dorm later."

Nina shrugged and, with a quick backward wave, headed for Dickenson Hall.

Elizabeth watched as Nina crossed the quad, walking right past the two dark-haired girls. She never gave them a glance. Elizabeth shook her head. *I'm just being paranoid,* she told herself. *If it was actually Gin-Yung, Nina would have noticed.*

Turning on her heel, Elizabeth headed toward WSVU. She really *did* have to stop by the television station—she had only been avoiding it because she didn't want to run into Tom. But when faced with the choice of either going to WSVU or finding out who those two mysterious girls were, the former seemed only slightly less nerve-racking.

As Elizabeth walked, she couldn't stop herself from shooting furtive glances over her shoulder toward the two faraway girls with the blue-black hair. *Well, what if Gin-Yung really was back in town?* Elizabeth taunted herself. *What would that mean for you and Todd?*

Elizabeth thrust the idea from her mind and vowed not to tell Todd about what she saw. Gin-Yung's return was one possibility that she and Todd didn't need to think about—not quite yet.

Chapter
Three

Jessica whipped the red Jeep Cherokee that she and Elizabeth shared into a fifteen-minute parking zone in front of the police station.

With its huge plate-glass windows and polished stone exterior, the building looked more like a boutique than a police station. Except there were no mannequins in the windows, no stylishly arranged fashions . . . just cops.

Jessica giggled to herself. *A cop mall. A policeman superstore. Walk right in, pick out a strong, handsome policeman, and charge him to your parents' credit card.* The thought made her snort out loud.

And we do have quite a selection today, she thought as she stepped through the wide glass doors into a room that simply teemed with all shapes and sizes of muscular, uniformed policemen.

There were women police officers too, of course, but Jessica somehow didn't seem to notice them.

A dark-eyed, tan policeman whose muscles practically burst through a T-shirt that read PO-LICE smiled as he passed her. Although he wasn't as gorgeous as Nick, he was every bit as good-looking as Bobby Hornet. In fact, he sort of reminded her of Bobby, except with just a bit more of a good-guy attitude.

Yes, quite a selection, she thought. *All just standing around, waiting to be picked.*

A policewoman with her hair pulled back in a tight chignon approached. "Can I help you?" she asked.

Jessica took a deep breath and was tempted to reply, "Not at the moment. I'm just browsing." But she swallowed that response and calmly said, "No, thanks, I'm just here to see Nick Fox."

The woman smiled stiffly, and Jessica continued through the busy police station as if she owned the place. She passed the waiting area lined with orange plastic chairs—not to mention a few creepy-looking characters—and turned left down a long, gray-green hallway.

She wasn't *really* browsing, of course. She had already made her selection. And she had chosen the best police officer in the cop super-store. How could she possibly want *anyone* else when she had Nick Fox?

But when she reached the door to the detectives' room, she paused. *Stop acting like a boy-crazy fool and get a grip,* she told herself. *All the distractions in the world won't change the reason why you came. Remember, you're here to talk to Nick about the charity calendar, not to admire his gorgeous coworkers.*

Jessica shook her hands loosely at her sides like a swimmer preparing for a race and opened the door. A shrill wolf whistle brought everyone's attention to the doorway. Jessica forgot herself for a moment and basked in the glow.

She flicked a strand of blond hair over her shoulder and struck a pose. "Is Nick here?" she asked.

"Hey, Nick," yelled Dub Harrison, a short, beefy detective who smelled like a cigar. "Some sorority babe to see you. Probably needs a rent-a-cop to chaperone her spring formal."

"Nice to see you too, Dub." Jessica knew all about Dub. Nick called him the king of practical jokers.

"Maybe she needs a date to the policeman's ball," someone else suggested.

"Hey, honey, if Nick's busy, I'm available!" Dub offered.

A few good-natured catcalls and whistles chimed around the room as Nick rushed over to greet her. She kissed him right in front of everyone.

Dub hooted. The tall, thin detective at the third desk made loud kissing noises.

"Knock it off, you guys," Nick said, ushering Jessica to his desk in the corner.

Nick's desk was separated from the other desks by a low partition and a couple of potted ferns. Sunlight from the room's only window glinted off the plaques and commendations hanging on the wall over his desk.

Nick lifted a huge stack of files from the extra chair and dumped them atop an overloaded file cabinet, but Jessica had already flopped into Nick's desk chair and was swiveling in circles.

"You'll never guess why I'm here," she said, stopping the spinning chair with an outstretched leg against his desk.

"You haven't crashed into my mother again, have you?"

Jessica rolled her eyes. "Don't joke about that, Nick," she warned, remembering the unfortunate accident that had nearly gotten her off on the wrong foot with his parents. While hurrying to meet the Foxes for dinner, Jessica had rear-ended Mrs. Fox's brand-new Lexus and gotten in a screaming match with her—without realizing who she really was. They eventually got the misunderstanding straightened out, but for a while it seemed as if Jessica had ruined everything between her and Nick.

"Well, why else would you need a cop?"

"I'm always in need of one cop in particular," Jessica purred as Nick leaned over her, tilting the desk chair backward in the process.

"I'm always at your service."

Jessica could smell Nick's cologne and feel the warmth of his breath on her face. Gently he took her chin in one hand and kissed her. Already off-balance in the tilted chair, Jessica felt as if she were falling. Her arms and legs jerked instinctively.

Nick backed away only an inch or two and grinned. "Don't worry. I wouldn't let you fall, Jess. Trust me."

"Oh, I do." She ran her fingers through his dark brown hair. He'd worn it long when he had been working undercover on campus. Now it was neatly trimmed to a more regulation length, but it was still thick and soft. He leaned forward again and nuzzled her neck.

"Whoa," she said, scooting out from under him and jumping out of the chair. "I don't want to get you fired."

Nick practically fell face first into the chair she'd just vacated. "It might be worth it," he murmured, regaining his balance and turning around.

Giggling mischievously, Jessica pushed Nick

into his own chair and leaned against his desk.

"You look gorgeous, Jessica. I love that beige miniskirt."

"It's not beige; it's ecru."

"Oh, excuse me. As a cop, I should be more discriminating with my descriptions."

Jessica's heartbeat sped up a bit. She loved it when she and Nick got into fast-paced teasing like this. "Yes, I'd say you do need to work on your powers of observation."

"Oh, my powers of observation are outstanding," Nick assured her huskily, "but what I was actually observing were those long, tan legs below that miniskirt. Tan *is* the correct shade of your legs, am I correct?"

She shifted slightly, tugging on the end of her skirt. "Cut it out, Nick. You're making me forget why I'm here."

"Well, did you come to brighten up my otherwise dull day, or does your visit have something to do with that very delicious-smelling white sack you tossed on my desk?"

Jessica smiled and reached for the sack. "I hope you're hungry."

"Famished!"

She unrolled the top of the sack. "I brought you a giant sandwich from Ruma's Deli. It's your favorite—smoked turkey and Swiss on French bread."

"With spicy mustard?"

"*Lots* of spicy mustard."

"You're the greatest."

Jessica beamed. "What's that again? I didn't hear you."

"You heard me, sunshine."

"OK, I heard you." She perused Nick's messy desk. "What have you been up to today?"

"I've just been working on these stupid files," Nick said. He took a bite of the sandwich and let out a throaty groan. "Oh, Jess, this is incredible. I've had nothing but Dub's coffee since eight this morning."

A stained Tazmanian Devil mug sat amid the piles of file folders on Nick's desk. Jessica turned up her nose at the vile-looking black goo lurking at the bottom.

"Here," she said, handing Nick a hot paper cup. "Lucky for you, I also brought you some *real* coffee."

"Shhh—don't let Dub hear you say that."

Jessica grabbed a napkin. "You have mustard on your chin. Here, let me." She dabbed at the spot and kissed it when she was through.

"Thanks. Aren't you going to join me?"

"No, I've already eaten."

"Good. I didn't really want to share."

Nick seemed to be so happy with his sandwich, Jessica figured he was sufficiently weakened for her to pop the big question. She cleared her throat and straightened her shoulders confidently. "Nick, as long as you're taking a little break from work, there's something I wanted to talk to you about."

"Um-hummm," Nick mumbled, his mouth full of sandwich.

"You know how my sister, Elizabeth, wants to be a journalist."

"Um-hummm."

"And Nina wants to be a physicist, and Todd wants to be a coach, and Isabella—"

"Stop right there." Nick wiped his mouth and took a drink of coffee. "Have you memorized the career goals of every student on campus?"

"Well, I'm just trying to make a point."

"And your point is?"

Jessica looked down at the floor and absently pushed a paper clip around with the toe of her shoe. "I think I'm the only one on campus who doesn't have a plan."

Nick put down his coffee cup. "Let me guess—you've decided on something?"

"How did you know?"

"My astute powers of observation. Remember? We've already discussed that." Nick grinned triumphantly, but his green eyes were gentle.

"Well, what would you think if I told you I wanted to be a model?"

51

"You've got the legs for it."

"*Seriously,* Nick."

"OK, seriously. I think you'd make a perfect model, Jessica. You're far prettier than any of the women I see in magazines or on TV—and I'm not just saying that because you're my girlfriend, all right? I mean it. You have a certain spark that goes way beyond physical beauty—and you're no slouch in that department either."

Jessica's heart swelled. "You really think I could do it?"

"I *know* you could. If I was a talent scout out looking for models, I'd sign you up in a second. What's this all about?"

"Well, see, they're making a calendar—SVU is anyway, and it's a charity thing to raise money for the homeless. And they want girls from different organizations on campus to model for it."

"And they picked you?"

"Yes. Well, no, not yet, but I'm pretty sure they will—if I tell them I want to do it, that is."

"So what are you waiting for? Go tell them you want to do it."

"But it's going to be a really sexy calendar. Bikinis on the beach—that sort of thing." Jessica bit her bottom lip. She'd made it this far, and she was silently praying that Nick wouldn't nix it at the last moment.

"Sounds like a great idea to me," he said casually.

Jessica was flabbergasted. "Are you *sure* you wouldn't mind? Because if you do, I'll forget all about it."

Nick reached over and took one of Jessica's hands in both of his. "Jessica, listen to me. You are more beautiful and confident than any other woman I have ever met. One of the things I love most about you is that you aren't afraid to show the world how gorgeous you are."

"But I'd be wearing a really sexy bikini," she said meekly.

"Do you honestly think I'd dislike seeing a picture of you in a sexy bikini?"

Jessica blushed. "But how would you feel about *everyone else* seeing it?"

Nick leaned back in his chair and smiled. "I'd be proud."

Instantly her eyebrows shot up. "You wouldn't be jealous knowing that other guys were going to hang your girlfriend's picture on their wall?" she asked incredulously.

"Jessica, not only wouldn't I be jealous—I'd hang one up on this very wall for every guy in this station to see." Nick pounded the wall above his desk for emphasis. "Let them eat their hearts out. Not only am I not afraid to show you off, I'd be *absolutely proud* to show you off."

Jessica squealed with joy and threw herself into Nick's lap. "I adore you—did you know that?"

Nick rubbed his nose against hers. "I got that idea a while back, but you can tell me again if you want."

"C'mere. I'll show you." She reeled him in for a long, passionate kiss, but they were interrupted by the ringing of Nick's phone.

"Nick, line two," Dub yelled. "It's Chief Wallace."

Nick held up a finger. "I have to take it," he said reluctantly.

"Then I'll let you get back to work," Jessica whispered, hopping out of his lap and leaving a silent kiss on his cheek. "Thanks, sweetie."

As Jessica walked—no, *floated*—out of the police station, she let out a huge sigh. Not only was Nick in favor of her being in the calendar, but all the great things he'd said about her made her feel as if she were glowing. She was feeling so good, in fact, that she figured it would be OK for her to bring up that little part about Bobby Hornet some other time. Like maybe after the calendars were already printed.

Skipping over to the Jeep, Jessica turned her face to the warm California sun. "What a boyfriend!" she shouted skyward. "Sexy, dangerous, adventurous . . . and supportive!"

Gin-Yung shivered and pulled her navy blue blazer more tightly around her. Even though it was buttoned, it still hung loosely. *None of my clothes fit me anymore,* she realized.

"Are you cold?" Kim asked.

"No, I'm fine." How could she explain to Kim that it wasn't the cool breeze or the lengthening shadows that were making her shiver? Gin-Yung was chilled by the fact that another day was ending. Another day had slipped through her fingers, making her feel cold and hollow inside.

In the two hours she and Kim had been sitting in the quad, countless students had rushed by without noticing them, as if they were merely parts of the scenery that they took for granted every day. *Slow down,* Gin-Yung longed to call out. *Take time to appreciate the small things in life. Don't overlook the beauty around you.*

Maybe sitting out on the quad *had* been a bad idea. Campus just didn't feel the same. Gin-Yung couldn't believe how a few months could make so much difference. Last semester she'd felt so at home at SVU. She'd had Todd, her friends, and her job at the newspaper. Now she felt like a total outsider—a stranger in the very place she'd counted on most to make her feel better about having to leave her internship in London and come back to Sweet Valley. It was almost as if all the students Gin-Yung knew had disappeared.

Gin-Yung had seen only one person she recognized all day—Winston Egbert. And he'd hardly stopped long enough to say hello. He'd been with three girls from his dorm, and they were all hurrying to get to class.

Why did it seem as if everyone was rushing to get someplace? What good was it? All it did was remind Gin-Yung that she had nowhere to go.

"I guess we ought to get moving," Gin-Yung said, looking up at the darkening sky. "It's getting late."

"Did you really think he would happen to just stroll by?" Kim asked confrontationally.

"What are you talking about?"

"Todd, of course. He's not going to just magically appear, Gin. You're going to have to make an effort to go find him."

"I told you last night. I'm not ready to see Todd just yet."

"Yeah, but you did say you were going to do it today. And all you've done is sit here on this stupid bench. Why do you keep putting it off, Gin? He's your boyfriend. He has a right to know you're back, even if you don't tell him . . . everything."

Gin-Yung stood up and dusted off the back of her khakis. A breeze whipped through the loose, baggy legs. "I'm ready to go home now. Are you coming?"

Kim rolled her eyes. "As long as we're already on campus, why don't you just drop by his dorm and say hi? I can go with you, or I can wait for you in the coffee shop."

A burning sensation ripped through Gin-Yung's stomach. "Aren't you listening to me at all?" she lashed out. "I didn't come here to see Todd. I simply wanted to sit in the sun and enjoy being back on campus for a while."

"'Enjoy,'" Kim mocked her. "That's a laugh."

Gin-Yung spun around and glared at her sister, her eyes blazing.

"Oh, Gin, I'm sorry—"

"That's it, Kim. I'm going home. Or maybe *you* want to go see Todd yourself, since that's all you can talk about. Would you like to meet me in the coffee shop afterward?"

"Gin-Yung, please, don't get angry."

"I'm not angry."

"Yes, you are, Gin! I know you are. I'm just—I'm just thinking about what's best for you, that's all. I don't want to see you sitting around and moping."

"Thanks, *Mom*, but why can't *I* decide what's best for me?"

"OK. I give up." Kim sighed, got up from the bench, and followed Gin-Yung without another word.

Gin-Yung pressed her lips together tightly.

Even though she didn't want to admit it, she knew that everything her sister said was true. Gin-Yung *had* hoped to "accidentally" bump into Todd today on the quad. It seemed as if a chance meeting might be best. But fate just wasn't on her side today. At any rate, she wasn't going to go to Todd's dorm room—not tonight. That somehow seemed too final, as if she'd be making a commitment that was greater than her own strength to follow through on it.

I'm not going to see Todd until the time is absolutely right, Gin-Yung vowed silently. She was in no hurry to face him—not yet anyway. Because when she did, Gin-Yung knew she'd have no choice but to tell him the truth about her return to Sweet Valley. And she didn't want to rush into a reunion that would turn out to be awkward, horrible, and terribly, terribly sad.

Chapter Four

"Hey, are you ready?" Todd asked brightly when Elizabeth opened the door to room 28, Dickenson Hall. But when he didn't see her smile, his spirits sank. "What's wrong? Am I too early?"

"No, you're right on time." Elizabeth peered out into the hallway as if she expected someone else to be there. "I'm all set," she said briskly. "Just let me grab my purse."

"You're sure nothing is wrong?"

"I'm sure."

No, something *was* wrong—Todd could feel it. *Maybe she's just tired,* he thought. Todd knew she had a rough class load on Thursdays. He decided to try teasing her out of her mood.

"I bet I know what's wrong," he kidded.

"What?" Elizabeth asked, sounding a little too surprised for Todd's comfort.

"Well, you must be disappointed that we're going to a boring old concert. I know how much you hate music. I'm sure you'd rather be going to a ball game, or maybe you'd just prefer to go somewhere and watch paint dry." Todd smiled good-naturedly.

Elizabeth's shoulders relaxed a little, and her blue-green eyes brightened.

Heartened, Todd continued. "But my bio lab partner practically *shoved* these two tickets down my throat, and she made me *promise* to show up. I guess they've been having trouble filling the Fine Arts Center lately."

Elizabeth chuckled softly. "That's because too many students are off watching you jocks."

"Well, people know what they like, I guess," Todd said, warming up even more when he saw Elizabeth's dimple appear.

"True. I know what I like."

"Me too." He leaned over and kissed her on the tip of her nose.

"Hey—you missed," Elizabeth deadpanned.

"Then please, let me try again," Todd said, taking Elizabeth by the shoulders and kissing her firmly on the lips.

"That's better," she said when he broke away. "From now on, Todd, I want you to kiss me like you did last night."

"Last night?" He slapped his forehead in

mock surprise. "Was that *you* I was with last night?"

Elizabeth laughed as she ran to the stairwell. She hurried down the stairs ahead of him, her blond ponytail bobbing in time to her steps.

This is more like it, Todd thought. He'd known for a long time that while he and Elizabeth were broken up, he never quite felt complete. Even while he was dating Gin-Yung, a part of him longed to be with Elizabeth. And now that they were back together, it was almost as if he'd been reborn.

When Elizabeth came to Todd's room last Friday night and told him that she wanted to be with him for good, they'd held each other for what seemed like hours and swore they'd never let each other go. Todd had thought then that it would turn out to be the best night of his life.

But last night surpassed it completely. The dinner had been incredible. And the good-night kiss—unbelievable. It was the perfect new beginning for the both of them. When he got back to his room, he'd hardly been able to sleep a wink. But that didn't even matter. Being with Elizabeth filled Todd with an energy he couldn't describe—or live without.

When they reached the Dickenson Hall lobby, Todd opened the door for Elizabeth, and together they stepped out into the cool evening

61

air. A group of students sat on the grass nearby, talking and listening to music.

Todd waved at a dark-haired girl from his English class, then turned back to Elizabeth. He was startled to see that her face seemed a bit wistful again.

"Really, Elizabeth. We don't have to go to this thing if you don't want to. Just say the word."

"No, I'm fine. Really. I'm glad we're going to a concert," Elizabeth insisted as they headed across the quad. "The university orchestra is really good this year."

"This won't be the whole orchestra. Just strings, I think. Some sort of recital they have to do for class."

"Well, I'm sure it'll be more interesting than some old ball game," she teased. "Besides, if it was a game, I'd have to sit alone in the stands and watch you play. This way I can have you right next to me."

She slipped her arm around his waist and leaned closer, but they hadn't gone many steps before she stiffened and pulled away.

Todd's chest deflated. Why was she acting this way?

"Elizabeth, what's the matter? One minute you're smiling, and the next you're frowning off into space somewhere."

"Sorry."

Todd groaned softly and stopped walking. "Please, Liz. Don't I deserve a better answer than 'sorry'? What's wrong?"

Elizabeth whirled around, her eyes flashing defiantly. "Nothing's wrong."

"Are you feeling sick?"

"*No*. Come on, Todd. I hate being late to concerts. It's so rude to walk in after they've already begun."

Todd shook his head. "I know I'm acting childish, but I'm not budging until you tell me what's wrong."

"*Nothing*."

"Elizabeth, we've known each other for far too long for you to pull something like this. It's not Watts again, is it? Did he do something else? Because if he did—"

"N-No."

Todd rolled his eyes and turned Elizabeth to face him. He put his hands on her shoulders and lowered his head down to hers. "Tell me, Liz."

"OK," she relented with a sigh. "I *did* see Tom at the TV station today, but only for a second. It was nothing, really. I just turned around and walked out. It was silly."

"Not if it ruins your whole day."

Elizabeth shrugged. "I'll get over it. I'll just have to make sure I only go to WSVU when he's not going to be there."

"That won't be easy, Liz. You know as well as I do that Watts is there practically twenty-four hours a day."

"Maybe." Elizabeth seemed to drift off for a second, then she firmly met his gaze. "Look, let's just go to the concert, OK?" She didn't wait for an answer—just turned and started back along the sidewalk.

It was clear she didn't want to talk about Tom anymore, but Todd wanted Elizabeth to know that she didn't have to hide anything from him—no matter what it was. Besides, he was getting really tired of hearing about—and seeing—all the new ways in which Tom Watts made Elizabeth's life miserable.

Todd caught up with Elizabeth in a couple of long-legged strides and took her hand. "Don't jump on me for saying this," he began hesitantly. "But . . . maybe you should consider quitting the station."

Elizabeth's eyes widened. "Quit my work at WSVU! Todd, I *couldn't*. Reporting is the only thing that keeps me sane half the time. I *need* my job at WSVU. Besides, I'm *good* at it. It's what I want to do. I can't let Tom Watts affect my entire career plan. I'll just have to learn to cope with seeing him around, that's all."

Todd stroked her arm, hoping to calm her down. "I didn't mean for you to quit reporting.

I know how much you love it. But newspapers were your first love, remember? You loved being editor of the *Oracle* back in high school. Your number-one goal when we started college was to become the editor of the *Sweet Valley Gazette*."

Elizabeth nodded solemnly.

"I remember how upset you were when we first got here and you couldn't get into Journalism I."

Elizabeth put her hands on her hips. "I'm surprised you remember *anything* I said to you during those first few weeks we were at school."

"What?" Todd blurted, shocked. "What's gotten into you, Elizabeth? I thought we were way past all that. Yes, I was a selfish jerk when we first came to college. I had a swelled head, an out-of-control ego, and I messed up everything. How many times do I have to apologize?" Todd's tirade spilled out so quickly, he found himself gasping for air.

Weakly Elizabeth covered her face with her hands. "I'm sorry. I don't know what made me bring that up."

"We have to put all that behind us, Liz." Todd wrapped his arms around her and shook his head sadly. "We wouldn't be here right now if we weren't willing to do that. It's our future that's important . . . our future together."

She sighed against his chest. "You're

right. Let's just forget everything I said."

Todd kissed the top of Elizabeth's head. "I'm not sure we should—not if something's bothering you in the back of your mind. Do you think the past is going to creep up on us and ruin everything?"

Elizabeth jolted in his arms and looked up at him with fear in her eyes. "No!" she gasped.

"Then let's forget about it for tonight," Todd said soothingly. "Let's forget our first breakup. Let's forget Tom, and WSVU, and schoolwork, and ball practice, and anything else that doesn't have anything to do with you, me, and the concert that's going to be starting in about three minutes. OK?"

"OK." Elizabeth sniffed. "I'm sorry, Todd. I guess I'm just in a weird mood tonight."

"Don't worry about it," Todd said, giving her a quick kiss. "Let's go."

Todd held out his hand, and Elizabeth took it. As they walked toward the Fine Arts Center Elizabeth would smile up at him occasionally, but something still didn't seem right. Every once in a while Elizabeth's eyes would dart around furtively, as if she expected someone to leap out of the bushes at them. She seemed jumpy, almost paranoid.

She's doing it again, Todd thought. *Looking around every corner, tensing at every movement.*

She's afraid we're going to bump into Tom Watts.

Todd couldn't blame Elizabeth for feeling that way. He had seen what could happen when Tom got anywhere near Elizabeth—his nasty sneer, the vicious taunts and name-calling. Todd shuddered just thinking about it.

Watts can go hang for all I care, Todd thought. *Elizabeth has me to protect her now. Tom Watts would be wise to keep himself far out of sight.*

I knew we'd be late, Elizabeth thought exasperatedly as she and Todd groped their way to their seats in the dark. *But it's my own fault. I shouldn't have let Todd see me acting so weird.*

They sank into their seats just as the curtains opened. Elizabeth sat stick straight and applauded along with the audience. But when the glorious sound of a Mozart concerto began to fill the Fine Arts Center, Elizabeth finally allowed herself to sit back and relax.

She leaned closer to Todd, whose arm was draped firmly around her shoulders. She could feel the warmth of his body and smell his cologne. It was the same cologne he'd always worn in high school. The smell conjured up so many happy memories for her.

Elizabeth closed her eyes, letting her thoughts drift along with the music. She and

Todd had made the perfect couple in high school. Nothing could stop them. Now she had a chance to reclaim the same contentment she'd had back then. Elizabeth smiled as she envisioned the moment at Rue Lafayette when Todd pulled the single red rose from under his jacket and held it out to her, his brown eyes glowing. *Am I going to spoil my second chance with Todd by letting myself believe that I might have seen Gin-Yung today?* she asked herself. *No. I'd be crazy to.*

She glanced up at Todd. He looked just as handsome in his casual knit polo shirt and Levi's as he had in his suit the night before. Maybe even more so.

Just then Todd glanced down, caught her looking at him, and grinned. He moved his arm from behind her, and in the semidarkness she felt his fingers twine with hers.

"I love you," she whispered.

He lifted her hand to his lips and kissed it in response.

As she rested her head on Todd's shoulder Elizabeth silently hoped Todd wasn't upset at her for bringing up Tom Watts like that. She felt a twinge of guilt about using her ex-boyfriend as an excuse for her strange behavior. But she hadn't lied—not exactly. She *did* see Tom at the station, but that wasn't the real reason she'd been so uptight on the way over. She didn't dare tell Todd what had really been bothering her all evening.

How could she possibly explain to Todd that she'd actually expected to see Gin-Yung with every footstep? Maybe she *should* tell Todd that she had seen a girl who looked a lot like Gin-Yung on the quad today. Maybe . . . later. Right now, as a lovely cello solo began, it didn't matter. Because the solo was so beautiful, it swept all her troubles away, leaving Elizabeth completely immersed in the love and joy she felt at having Todd beside her.

It feels good to stretch my legs, Tom Watts thought as he stood in the cramped backstage area with the string players, their parents, and other well-wishers. He leaned back against the wall and felt the bones of his spine crackle. The recital *had* seemed a little long—but maybe it was having to sit through the whole thing alone that made it seem that way.

Still, Dana's solo had made it all worthwhile. Her performance had been so tender and sad, it had brought tears to Tom's eyes. But then, a lot of things had brought tears to Tom's eyes lately.

"Hey, Wildman!" Brett Ryder yelled. Brett was a football player and casual friend from Tom's freshman year.

Brett bulldozed his way in Tom's direction,

scrambling over the two rows of folding chairs and knocking over a music stand, sending loose pages in a flutter behind him. Brett didn't seem to notice— or care.

"Since when did you become a classical music fan, buddy?" Brett asked, clamping a hand on Tom's shoulder. "Or are you like me— getting dragged here by your girlfriend? Where is Liz anyway?"

Tom held back the growl that was rising in his throat. Why couldn't anyone let him forget? "I'm not with her," he said with a snarl. "We aren't together anymore."

"Oh? I hadn't heard," Brett said indifferently. "Why are you here, then? Covering the concert for the station?"

"No, I'm here with Dana Upshaw, the cellist. We're dating now."

Brett didn't seem to be impressed one way or the other. "Where've you been hiding out? I haven't seen you since the last Delta Chi party, man. We've missed you."

Tom winced at the mention of that embarrassing night at Delta Chi. He had made a complete fool of himself with his drinking and womanizing—not to mention the fact that he almost got into a fight with his best friend and roommate, Danny Wyatt.

"I've been busy," Tom said, keeping an eye out for Dana.

"Dude, was that a wild bash or what? You were definitely the chugalug champ that night! We all knew you still had it in you!"

"Not for long, I didn't." Tom felt nauseous as he remembered the miserable hours he'd spent after the party hugging the commode, but his comment whizzed right over Brett's head.

"Oh, man, you lie. You know you can still hang with the best. The Wildman *rules!*" Brett raised his fist in the air obnoxiously.

Tom smiled as politely as he could, desperately hoping Dana would show up and rescue him.

"All righty, then!" Brett smacked his beefy hands together loudly. "Look, why don't you and Dina—"

"Dana."

"—join Pammy and me? We're heading for the Delta Phi house."

"No, thanks, Brett. Not tonight."

"It's going to be major. A five-kegger."

"Naw, I don't think Dana would be up for it."

"Well, maybe you can stop by after you ditch the wet blanket."

Tom glared at Brett. "I said thanks, but no thanks," he snarled through his teeth.

"I get it. The old lady doesn't want you partying, eh?"

No, you don't get it at all, Tom thought with an internal groan. But he was willing to let Brett believe whatever he wanted, just as long as he went away before Dana arrived. Brett was so clueless, he might end up making another comment about . . . that *other* girl.

"OK, maybe next time," Brett said, clearly unfazed. "Catch you later, Wildman."

Tom heaved a sigh of relief as he watched Brett shove his way out the backstage exit. *Sorry, Brett. Not this time. Not next time. Not anytime,* Tom thought. *You caught the one and only command performance of Wildman Watts.*

After Tom's painful breakup with . . . his ex, he had tried going back to his old Wildman persona. He'd thought that reviving his heavy-drinking, party-hardy quarterback image from freshman year would be the perfect way for him to make a clean break of things. But after letting himself get out of control at the Delta Chi party, not to mention the hangover he suffered through the next day, Tom realized that Wildman Watts was better left to the past, just as a lot of other things were. Times changed, and you had to go with the flow—or drown.

He knew he didn't want to be Wildman Watts, but he didn't want to go back to being Mr. Heart-on-his-sleeve either. Never again would he let himself be gullible enough to be duped by the next cruel little con artist who came along, smashing down his defenses with a flash of her big blue-green eyes and a toss of her long blond ponytail. Tom knew he had to change, but he just wasn't sure who he was supposed to be at this point.

Tom looked at his watch impatiently. If all else failed, he could always go to the station and get some work done. He'd only been to the station once in the past three days, and then he'd had the bad luck to run into *her*. Seeing her had upset him so much, he'd been unable to get anything accomplished.

"Tom! Oh, there you are! I've been looking all over for you."

Expectantly Tom looked up and saw Dana running toward him. Even though she was dressed in her required long black skirt and white blouse, Dana still managed to look unique. From the lace-up granny boots that peeked out from under her skirt to the sparkling rhinestone glasses that rested on her nose, she'd found several not-too-subtle ways to show off her individuality.

"How did you like the concert?" Dana asked breathlessly.

"It was great, Dana. But your solo . . . it was extreme! You were incredible. The star of the show."

"Thanks, Tom," she said, blushing. "I'm so glad you liked it." Suddenly Dana wrapped her arms around Tom and gave him a big, affectionate hug.

The hug took Tom by surprise, but he was even more surprised to feel himself hugging back. *This girl is something else,* Tom realized. *Not only is she gorgeous and talented, but she isn't afraid to show how she feels about me.* But just as he relaxed into the embrace, Dana abruptly pulled away.

"I'm so thrilled you could make it," she said. "I hope you enjoyed the program."

What is she doing? Tom thought. *Does she expect me to repeat everything I just said?* He started to answer, but just in time he realized she was looking over his shoulder and talking to someone behind him.

"We loved your solo, Dana," said a deep, familiar voice. "Don't take this the wrong way, but you're a lot more impressive onstage than you are in bio lab."

"Well, what can I say? Frogs just aren't my thing," Dana replied with a disarming smile.

Tom spun around to see Todd Wilkins—holding Elizabeth Wakefield's hand. Elizabeth immediately dropped Todd's hand as if it were a spider, but Todd simply took his free arm and possessively wrapped it around Elizabeth's waist. Tom seethed when Elizabeth didn't move from his grasp.

"Dana," Todd began, ignoring Tom completely, "have you met my girlfriend, Elizabeth Wakefield?"

Tom's heart sped uncontrollably. Unbelievable! It was one thing for Tom to bump into his ex at WSVU, but seeing her practically *attached* to Wilkins like that—it was too much.

The pounding in his temples drowned out the laughter and conversation around him. Tom turned away, his face stinging. He was too furious to see or hear a thing.

How could that woman be so heartless? he wondered. She was following him, taunting him, flaunting the fact that she was back with Todd Wilkins. She was probably doing it on purpose. *Well, two can play this little game,* Tom said silently. *I'll show you I'm not missing you either.*

Tom spun back around and forced himself to speak. "As I was saying, Dana, before we were interrupted"—he struggled to keep his voice at a normal pitch—"you were marvelous. You blew everyone away." He punctuated his sentence by stroking Dana's mahogany hair.

He quickly glanced toward Elizabeth to see her response, but her eyes were fixed on the floor. Then he turned back toward Dana. Dana stared up at him with wide innocent eyes, and for a second he thought he saw a smile of satisfaction on her face.

Did Dana plan to—no, don't be crazy, Tom told himself. The anger churning in his gut was making him see things. *Get a grip, Watts. Dana wouldn't do something like that.*

Tom looked again at Elizabeth. She seemed perfectly content in Wilkins's arms. Her eyes downcast. Angelic. Bewitching. He couldn't stand it. He'd do anything to get her out of his sight.

Impulsively, without another word, Tom turned to Dana and swept her up into his arms until her feet actually left the ground. He kissed her with all the passion he could muster.

Dana's body tensed with surprise, but that only lasted for a second. Immediately she relaxed in his arms and returned his kiss.

Go away, go away, go away, Tom yelled silently at Elizabeth Wakefield. *If there is such a thing as ESP, you will know I never want to see your face again.*

When the retreating sound of Elizabeth's quick footsteps and Todd's mumbled threats assured Tom that the happy couple had left, he eased Dana's feet back to the floor and gently pulled away.

He didn't expect to see the depth of emotion in Dana's hazel eyes. When she reached up and clasped both her hands behind his neck, he allowed his face to be pulled back down to hers. Wordlessly Dana kissed him. And Tom returned her kiss automatically, without thinking.

Why not? Tom thought. *It's beginning to feel right.*

When the backstage lights flickered, Tom opened

his eyes and broke away from the embrace. "OK, people, let's clear out," came a booming voice, followed by the impatient clap of a pair of hands.

Tom stared into Dana's eyes for a long moment, transfixed. Then, just as suddenly as they'd embraced, Tom blinked and ran his fingers through his hair, forcing himself to come out of his trance. "Listen, Dana, I have to work at the station tonight," Tom whispered urgently. "But I want to see you again . . . tomorrow."

"Whenever you want, Tom. Just call me," Dana replied with a dizzy smile, standing on her tiptoes to receive one last, long kiss.

Elizabeth ran blindly from the concert hall. The evening air felt cool on her wet cheeks. She couldn't believe that the woman who'd played that passionate cello solo was the same one she'd seen Tom with last week. *How can someone like that make Tom act so cold,* she thought as the scene she'd just witnessed replayed in her mind.

"Liz, wait up!" Todd's voice broke through the ringing in her ears. He had caught up with her and was gently trying to pull her to a stop.

She sank into the protection of his arms. "Oh, Todd," she sobbed. "I'm sorry. I'm so embarrassed. I shouldn't have run off like that, but—"

"It's OK, Liz." Todd stroked her hair soothingly. "I'm here. Tom's history."

Elizabeth sniffed as Todd reached down and wiped away her tears. "I've spoiled our whole night," she murmured.

"No, you haven't," Todd said. He caught Elizabeth under the chin and tilted her face up until her eyes met his. "You haven't ruined anything. Besides, the night isn't over yet."

"I shouldn't have let Tom's—um—presence bother me."

"*Presence?* Is that what you want to call it? It was a *performance*, Liz!" Todd held her out at arm's length. "Anyone could see that he was kissing Dana out of pure spite. He did it for one reason and one reason only—to hurt you."

Elizabeth looked down at the ground. "I guess you're right."

"Guess so? I *know* so," Todd said, kissing her cheek where a lone tear was falling. "Don't let Tom get to you, Liz. I know you can be strong—stronger than he is, obviously."

Elizabeth relaxed a bit as Todd gently stroked one of her eyebrows with the tip of his thumb. "Thanks, Todd. I really needed to hear that." A relieved smile began to form on her lips.

"Oh, your smile—" Todd didn't finish his sentence; he only gazed into her eyes lovingly, the warmth of his brown eyes melting all her sadness away. He leaned in and kissed her, strongly and sweetly.

As Elizabeth lost herself in his kiss she felt as though she and Todd had never been apart, as if her months spent with Tom Watts were all a bad dream. Now she was awake, and Todd was comforting her, helping her wipe the awful nightmare from her memory.

"Todd," Elizabeth began when they paused for breath, "you're right. Tom *is* history."

Smiling openly, Todd wrapped his arms around Elizabeth and held her tight. Elizabeth closed her eyes and listened to Todd's heartbeat. Was it true—was she really over Tom, once and for all?

A few weeks ago that backstage drama would have killed me, she realized. *But now I'm only annoyed—no, not even annoyed, just a little uncomfortable.* She sighed at her revelation.

"Are you OK, Liz?" Todd asked softly, releasing her from his grasp.

"Yes, I am," Elizabeth responded. "I really am."

"Are you sure? Because if you want me to, I can still go back in there and deck him."

Elizabeth wiped away the last of her tears with the back of her hand and laughed softly. "If I thought you were serious, I might just let you."

"I *am* serious."

"No, you're not." She shook her head and playfully tugged his hand. "Come on. Let's go for a walk."

"Maybe *you* feel better," Todd said after a few moments of walking in silence, "but I'm still steamed. I can't stand seeing you hurt, Liz."

She led him over to a concrete bench, and they sat down. "I'm all right, Todd. I just over-reacted, that's all."

"You say that now, but when I saw your face back there, it was like someone had stuck a knife in my heart. I wish there was something I could do to protect you."

"There is one thing," she whispered.

"What?"

"Hold me."

He took her in his strong arms. "How's this?"

"Perfect."

Todd kissed her hair. "We'll get through this together," he said quietly. "You and me. I love you, Liz."

"I love you too, Todd."

"You mean everything to me," he whis-pered, bending down and kissing her lips softly. "If you need to talk—even about Tom— I'll listen. Just don't shut me out like you did earlier tonight."

"Todd, I need you so much. Please . . . don't ever leave me."

"Of course I won't, Liz. Why would I ever want to?"

A flash of blue-black hair passed through

Elizabeth's mind. Involuntarily she began to sob again.

"Shhh, Liz. It's OK. I'm here," he whispered, holding her tight and stroking her hair.

Yes, Todd, you're here now, she thought, *but for how long? What if Gin-Yung comes back?*

Elizabeth shuddered at the thought. Maybe she had just been seeing things earlier today, but she knew that Gin-Yung wouldn't stay in London forever. How could Elizabeth stop him from going back to her?

I know one way. With conviction Elizabeth pulled Todd's face back down to hers. *If Todd can make me forget about Tom, then I can make him forget he* ever *had feelings for Gin-Yung Suh,* she vowed, pressing her lips to his.

Chapter Five

"Come *on*, Todd. Open up," Gin-Yung mumbled under her breath as she knocked on Todd's dorm-room door a third time. "I *know* you don't have classes this early. Don't make me give up now."

Gin-Yung could practically picture Todd snoozing away peacefully with a pillow over his head. Meanwhile she was wearing down her knuckles on his door.

After knocking one last time Gin-Yung stepped away. But she stopped in her tracks when she heard the doorknob turn.

The door swung open, and Todd's rumpled head appeared behind it. "Gin-Yung!" he gasped.

Todd was dressed in baggy sweatpants and a torn T-shirt, and his brown hair was sticking up. But beneath his sleepy-eyed expression was not a look of happy surprise, but one of genuine shock.

So much for my fantasy of running into his welcoming arms, she thought sullenly. *But I have to be strong. I won't get emotional. I won't fall apart.*

"Gin-Yung!" Todd repeated again, as if he were trying to wake himself up out of a dream. "Wh-What are you *doing* here? When did you get back?"

"Aren't you going to invite me in? Or are you going to give me the third degree out here in the hall?" Gin-Yung was surprised at how blank and emotionless her own voice sounded.

"Uh . . . sure. Come in." Todd stepped aside jerkily and held open the door. "Sit down," he said, knocking a pair of basketball shoes off his desk chair.

"Thanks." Gin-Yung sank gratefully into the chair. She felt tired, and her entire body quaked with anxiety. Looking around Todd's room, she was overcome with the same sensation she felt on the quad yesterday afternoon: the place felt familiar, yet completely unwelcoming.

Todd didn't say a word. He stood nervously, his face pale.

"Aren't you glad to see me?" Gin-Yung asked innocently.

"Of course I am," Todd insisted. But Gin-Yung could see his hands shaking slightly as he sank down onto his bed and faced her.

I guess I'm not getting a welcome-back kiss, Gin-Yung thought. *Not even a hug. But then again, maybe I wasn't really expecting one.*

"Wow," Todd said after a short, uncomfortable silence. "I can't believe it's really you. I thought you were going to be gone the rest of the year."

"Change of plans," Gin-Yung replied matter-of-factly.

"When did you get back?"

"Last Friday night."

"Last Friday night!" Todd anxiously ran a hand through his messy hair. "Why didn't you call me?"

Gin-Yung shrugged. "I've been meaning to, but I've been busy—you know, jet lag, unpacking, family things, stuff like that."

"What happened? Nothing went wrong with the internship, did it?"

"The internship was great." Gin-Yung's steely defenses were beginning to crumble. She longed to reach out and touch Todd, but he seemed to have an invisible barrier around him—one she wouldn't be able to break through.

"Nothing's wrong with your family, is it?"

"No, they're fine." Gin-Yung clasped her hands together in her lap tightly, trying to keep control of herself.

"Well, what's up?" Todd asked. "Don't make me do all the work here."

Work? Incensed, Gin-Yung drew in her breath sharply. *Does he really think that talking to me is* work? *An unpleasant chore, like taking out the garbage?* Tears began working their way to her eyes. She swallowed—too loudly. An embarrassing gulping sound echoed in her ears, but Todd didn't seem to notice. He just sat and stared, saying nothing.

"I'm home because—just because I wanted to come home, Todd. I was feeling homesick. I wanted to see everyone—my family, my friends. You." She watched Todd carefully for his response. A slight smile curved his lips, but it seemed more sad than cheerful.

"It must have cost you a bundle," Todd remarked, not meeting her eyes.

Gin-Yung tugged at a thread on the cuff of her oxford shirt. "It's worth it."

Todd drifted off in silence again, then cleared his throat. "So . . . when are you going back?"

A painful twinge shot up Gin-Yung's spine. "I'm not going back," she replied, sounding more angry than she wanted to.

"You mean you're home for good?" Todd's deep brown eyes were wide, disbelieving.

She nodded. "I'm back. For better or for worse." *That's an appropriate way to put it,* she thought bitterly.

"But the internship—that was a once-in-a-lifetime opportunity. And you loved London, didn't you?" Todd suddenly sounded energetic and urgent, as if he were desperate to convince Gin-Yung to go back to London forever.

"Well, you know, things change." *Lots of things change,* Gin-Yung thought, trying to find a way to break the truth to him gently. But she couldn't—not now. Todd already seemed to be in a state of shock; her news might not register with him.

It'll just have to wait, Gin-Yung realized as she watched Todd begin to nervously juggle a basketball between his hands. *Todd is obviously not ready to hear what I have to say. I'll give him some time to adjust to the fact that I'm back home, and then—I hope—he'll be ready to hear my secret. Because I have to tell him . . . before it's too late.*

Todd leaned against the closed door and let out a long, agonized groan. He couldn't believe it—Gin-Yung was back! He would have been less surprised to wake up and discover that his skin had turned green. But no, not today. Today he woke up to the sound of Gin-Yung Suh pounding at his door.

A pang of guilt grabbed at his chest, but he breathed through it, the same way he'd handle a muscle cramp. "I've done nothing to be ashamed of," he assured himself out loud. "We agreed to see other people while she was gone."

But now Gin-Yung is back, his conscience replied. *Gin-Yung is back, and you didn't tell her about Elizabeth.*

Todd shuddered. He *had* promised Elizabeth that he would tell Gin-Yung about their reunion as soon as he had a chance. But how could he have done that just now? He was half asleep and in a state of shock. Besides, it would have been a lot easier to tell her over the phone or in a letter. But with Gin-Yung right there in front of him . . . he couldn't have done it. Not just then anyway.

Anxiously Todd bolted over to the desk chair where Gin-Yung had just been sitting and picked up the polo shirt that had been draped over the back. It was the same shirt he had worn to the concert with Elizabeth the night before.

Todd held the shirt to his face and breathed in deeply. Yes—he could still smell Elizabeth's perfume on it. Had Gin-Yung noticed it? *What would Gin-Yung say if she knew I'd been with Elizabeth last night?* he wondered. *And what would Elizabeth say if she knew I was just talking to Gin-Yung—in my own room?*

"What am I going to do?" Todd moaned out loud, climbing back into his bed and hiding under his pillow. He felt sick—his thoughts spun around in circles, and so did his head. All he knew at this point was that he had to hurt one of the women in his life, or else he'd end up hurting them both.

"Here we are," Tom announced as he maneuvered his car around the winding, narrow driveway to the Seacliff Inn, home of the most expensive champagne brunch in southern California.

"Oh, Tom," Dana said. "It's gorgeous!"

When Tom pulled up in front of the door, two valets instantly sprang into action—one to take Tom's keys, and the other to help Dana out of the car. As Dana ooohed and aaahed some more, Tom grinned, glad that his date appreciated his good taste.

The Seacliff Inn was perfectly named. It was a quaint little cliff-top restaurant with startling views of the Pacific Ocean. Tom knew it was a class joint—his father, George Conroy, had brought him and his half siblings there for dinner one night. *George never stoops to anything second-rate*, Tom thought proudly.

The maitre d' greeted Tom by name as soon as they walked inside, and he led them back to the tables along the panoramic window.

"Look at the gorgeous yellow roses on that

table!" Dana exclaimed, pointing toward one of the tables. "There must be close to two dozen there."

There'd better be exactly *two dozen,* Tom thought.

Dana squealed when the maitre d' left them at the rose-laden table. She caressed a delicate blossom. "None of the other tables have roses. Do you think they're here by mistake?"

"Take a look at the card and see."

Dana eyed Tom mischievously as she plucked the card from the bouquet. "To Dana," she read aloud. "Me? These are for me!" She broke off a rose and tucked it behind her right ear. The delicate yellow bloom contrasted sharply with her mahogany hair and her patchwork calico dress. "Thank you, Tom. You're unbelievable. How did you know yellow roses are my favorite?"

"I took a wild guess," Tom remarked casually. He really hadn't, though; he had chosen them because they were just about the most expensive thing the florist had to offer.

Dana jumped up from her chair and rushed around the table to kiss him. Her lips were tender against his cheek.

A warm feeling of pride flowed through Tom's chest. He'd been out to impress, and he had succeeded. The bouquet alone cost more than what he had usually spent on Eliz—that other girl—in a month. She would have been unable to enjoy the flowers for worrying about what they cost.

Of course the old Tom would have worried about the same thing. It'd been tough paying his own way through school, especially after his mother and adoptive father were tragically killed in a car accident. But lack of money was a worry of the past, ever since he was found by his biological father, George Conroy. Mr. Conroy had set up a very generous trust fund for Tom's education. Tom found that his new attitude toward cash was a lot easier to live with. After all, what was it for if not to spend?

When a waitress presented them with a chilled bottle of champagne and told them to help themselves to the buffet table, Tom and Dana eagerly followed her instructions.

Tom's mouth watered as he looked over the sumptuous buffet. He hardly knew where to begin. There was plenty of fresh fruit and exotic breads and muffins. But there were steam trays heaped with more substantial dishes too. Tom couldn't make up his mind. French toast? Hash browns? Country ham? How about lobster quiche, with a side of prime-rib hash?

Dana was heaping strawberries and whipped cream onto a plateful of Belgian waffles. Tom couldn't help but remember how content his ex-girlfriend would have been with a plain bagel and a glass of orange juice. Well, it was her tough luck if she was always willing to settle for something less. He wasn't, not anymore. From now on it was only first class for Tom Watts.

After he scooped an enormous serving of eggs Benedict onto his crowded plate he followed Dana back to the table.

"What a view," Dana breathed as she looked out at the ocean. Tom jumped with surprise when he felt Dana's foot brush against his under the table. When he looked up to see if she'd meant to do that, her hazel eyes sparkled as they met his own.

"Isn't this romantic?" she whispered.

"Extremely," Tom agreed.

"I love it here. Let's stay until they throw us out."

He looked at their two heaping plates. If they stayed long enough to eat all the food they'd selected, it might very well take all day.

Dana forked a large strawberry and held it in front of Tom's lips. "Here. Taste it."

Tom took the strawberry, but he had to admit that Dana's full red lips looked a lot more inviting.

"Let's make a toast." He filled their glasses with champagne. "To us," he said, clinking his glass gently against hers.

"I'll drink to that," she said, sipping her

champagne demurely. "You know, Tom, this is our third official date, but I still don't know all that much about how you and the Conroys got together." Dana tapped her finger on the edge of her champagne glass. "I was really surprised that day I met you at their condo. I didn't realize you were the son that George had been looking for."

"Well, I grew up believing that my adoptive father was my real father. I never knew George Conroy existed until my twenty-first birthday."

"Wow, that's wild! It's like a movie of the week or something. How did he find you?"

"George had made a deal with my mother to stay out of my life until I was twenty-one. Then over the years he completely lost contact with us. But he still wanted to meet me. His search led him to SVU, and eventually we were introduced."

Tom left out the fact that it was his ex-girlfriend who'd discovered that George Conroy was Tom's real father and that she had been the one who'd done the introducing. And then she'd betrayed them both with her disgusting accusations—that his own father came on to her, with Tom sitting right there the whole time. . . .

But just when all the horrible memories of Tom's last relationship threatened to overtake him, he shoved them away quickly. Tom refused to let his perfect date be spoiled. That other girl clearly didn't need him anymore—and he didn't need her either. Because the beautiful woman sitting across from him was so perfect, so right for him, that he'd be crazy to think about anything other than her right now.

"I'm so glad George found you," Dana said. "Otherwise we might not have ever met."

"I'm glad too," Tom replied, and for once he was sure that he might actually have meant it.

"Hey! Egbert!" Todd called, running over to the Oakley Hall parking lot, where Winston was soaping down his beat-up Volkswagen. "Nice threads, buddy." Only Winston could get away with wearing plaid walking shorts and a retro polka-dot camp shirt at the same time.

With sponge in hand, Winston jumped away from the Bug and struck an exaggerated male-model pose. "Sorry, Todd, but I've been too busy to make it over to Jockland."

"Ha ha. Say, do you *really* think it'll help to wash this hunk of junk?" Todd kidded.

"Hey, Todd, don't laugh," Winston replied mock seriously. "When I'm finished, you'll think you're looking at a Porsche."

"There's not enough beer at Sigma house to make me think this is a Porsche."

Winston threw his soapy sponge in Todd's direction, but—typical of Winston's athletic prowess—he missed by a mile.

"Say, do you have a sec?" Todd asked. "I need to tell you something."

"Sure. Grab a rag, and we'll talk as long as your arm holds out."

Todd grabbed a torn T-shirt that had been soaking in a bucket of soapy water and started to scrub the bright orange roof. He decided not to beat around the bush. "Gin-Yung is back."

"I know. I saw her yesterday on my way to astronomy. She was sitting in the quad with her big sister."

"You saw her yesterday?" Todd exclaimed. "Why didn't you say something, man?"

"I said hello, but I didn't have time to chat."

Todd flicked soapy water in Winston's direction. "I mean, why didn't you say something to *me*—about her being back."

Winston shrugged. "I figured you knew."

"Well, I didn't," he admitted. "Not until she showed up at my dorm room first thing this morning."

"Bummer," Winston said, squatting down to scrub a tire.

"It's not a joke, Winston. You know, Gin and I never broke up—not officially."

Winston suddenly sprang to his feet. "But I thought you and Elizabeth were back together."

"We are. I mean, we were. I mean—"

"Oh, I get it," Winston said with a roll of his eyes. "Bummer."

"Look, this is how I see it. Whatever it was that Gin and I had has been over a long time. I just don't know how she feels, though. If I told her about me and Liz, it could really hurt her. Then again, maybe I don't have to tell her anything. Maybe Liz is the one I should be having the big talk with."

"Bum—"

"If you say 'bummer' one more time, I'm going to throw this nasty rag in your face!"

Winston pinched his lips together with his fingers and shook his head pleadingly.

"I'm begging for some advice here, Egbert. What should I do?"

Winston paused long enough to wipe water spots from his glasses. "Listen. I know what you want me to say. You want me to tell you to stick with Liz. And I want to. I think she's the greatest. I'd punch you out myself if I thought you were going to do something to hurt her again. Of course, I'd probably get killed in the process."

"Probably," Todd agreed good-naturedly. He knew how loyal Winston was to both Wakefield twins. And he couldn't blame Winston for his threat, however lighthearted it might have been. If Todd broke Elizabeth's heart again, he'd deserve whatever he got.

Winston scrubbed the rear fender of the Bug thoughtfully. "You know, living in an all-women's dorm has been a truly unique experience. I hear all these breakup and get-together stories from the girls' viewpoint, and it's made me see things in a different light."

Todd nodded for him to continue.

"Somebody is going to get hurt in this situation, no matter which way you go."

"My thoughts exactly."

"You're just going to have to talk to Gin-Yung and get your feelings out in the open. Tell her you want to break up with her, but be as gentle as you can. Be honest. You owe her that much, at least. She hasn't done anything wrong here. And she's always stuck by you."

Winston's right about that, Todd realized, shaking his head sadly.

"If you can't do that, then I think the only fair thing for you to do would be to call things off with Elizabeth."

"But it would kill me to do that—not to mention what it could do to Liz. You know I've loved her forever. But then again, you're right about Gin-Yung. She's a great girl. Man, I'm so depressed."

"Now, let me get this straight. You're depressed because you have two girls in love with you? I always knew I should have been a super-jock instead of the brilliant, sensitive type."

"Get real, Egbert!"

"No, really, I mean it! You've got to face the challenge head-on, Wilkins. Talk to Gin-Yung. Talk to Elizabeth. And be honest with both of them."

"Oh, man, I was hoping you'd have a better solution. I've already said all that to myself a hundred times."

"Well, you get what you pay for," Winston teased. "You know, I never thought I'd see the day when ol' Wherefore-art-thou-Romeo would come to me with his women troubles."

"Thanks a lot," Todd said, dipping his rag into the bucket. "I'm right back where I started from."

"Bummer," Winston said, raising his eyebrows tauntingly.

"I warned you!" With that Todd threw his soapy rag flat into Winston's face.

"Ugh!" Winston grabbed the water hose. "Take *that!*" he shouted triumphantly, turning on the spray. Todd got only half soaked before the water pressure from the hose made it jump from Winston's hands.

When Winston turned his back to scramble for the hose, Todd snatched up the bucket of soapy water and snuck up behind him. The water war of the century was now officially under way.

*　　　*　　　*

Jessica stomped on the brakes and whipped the Jeep into the only vacant parking space she could find. She wasn't as close to Disc-Oh! Music as she'd hoped, but it would have to do. Thanks to the arrival of Bobby Hornet, all the streets around the store were jammed with traffic.

She leaned toward the rearview mirror and checked her lipstick. *Perfect,* she thought. It matched her Racy Red nails exactly. She admired her fresh manicure, glad that Isabella had been able to redo her nails at the last minute. That pale peach just wouldn't do—not for what she had planned for this afternoon anyway.

Jessica quickly reapplied mascara to her long lashes, then covered her eyes with Nick's huge wraparound sunglasses. She puckered up her lips at her own reflection and smiled. "On your mark, get set, you *go,* girl!" she told herself before throwing her makeup bag in the glove compartment and snapping it shut.

Jumping stealthily from the Jeep, Jessica flipped up the collar of the long tan trench coat that practically covered her from head to toe. *I just knew that Nick would have the perfect undercover gear,* she thought as she tipped his sunglasses down her nose and peered over them. *I just hope he doesn't notice that this stuff is missing from his closet.* She cased the area, just like she'd seen countless female spies do in the old thriller movies she loved.

Satisfied that she hadn't been spotted by any evil-doing sorority sisters—well, one Theta sister in particular—Jessica sneaked around the corner and headed for the music store, making sure she kept close to the buildings. She longed for some shadows to weave in and out of, but they were hard to come by in the middle of a sunny Friday afternoon.

The nearer she got to Disc-Oh! Music, the more crowded the sidewalks became, and the more nervous and excited Jessica grew. No one seemed to take notice of her as she wedged her way through the crowd of fans that had gathered on the sidewalk directly in front of the record store. *They think I'm all innocent and harmless,* she realized. *Boy, will I show them.*

Once she pushed her way to the front window, she peeked inside the store. It was totally swamped. The majority of the crowd appeared to be made up of college girls armed with Polaroid pictures, snapshots, and even eight-by-ten glossies of themselves in bikinis.

In the very center of the main floor she caught a glimpse of Bobby Hornet's leather-clad back. His long, wavy, darkest brown hair was unmistakable. He was perched on a tall stool behind a specially decorated table, talking to people, looking at photos, and signing autographs.

What she saw next turned her stomach—the sight of Alison Quinn hovering nearby, her chemically tanned legs sticking out from underneath her madras shorts like two brown, knobby sticks. *No competition there,* Jessica thought proudly. *This is going to be like taking candy from a baby.*

Jessica took a deep breath, wet her lips, and smoothed down her blond bangs confidently before she slipped through the door, fashionably late—just as she'd planned.

Since everyone in the store was clamoring for Bobby's attention, Jessica was able to silently, sneakily climb up the long staircase to the classical music section without being spotted by anyone. Except for a couple of photographers who were snapping shots of Bobby through telephoto lenses, the entire upstairs balcony was deserted—and that suited Jessica just fine. *Ignore me now, while you still can!* she wanted to shout. As far as she was concerned everything was moving along like clockwork.

She moved to the center of the balcony and grasped the railing that overlooked the main part of the store. *Time for action,* she thought, removing Nick's sunglasses and stowing them away safely in one of the buttoned trench coat pockets. *Sweet Valley, you won't know what hit you.* Directly below her she could see the top of Bobby Hornet's head. *I hope you're ready for this, Mr. Rock Star.*

100

Quietly, with as little wasted motion as possible, Jessica unbuttoned the trench coat meticulously, one button after the other. When she finished, she slipped out of the coat, barely noticing when the store's air-conditioning raised goose bumps on her bare skin. After making some final adjustments to herself, Jessica leaned forward and dangled the trench coat over the railing— directly above Bobby Hornet's gorgeous mane.

"Whoops!" she gasped loudly as she let the coat go. It ballooned out and fluttered down, landing right across Bobby's table. Jessica put her hands up to her mouth as if she'd just made a horrible faux pas. "Oh, how clumsy of me!"

Faces whirled around and turned upward. Jaws dropped. The store went completely silent and drew in its collective breath. Even the background music came to a halt as everyone gaped up at the gorgeous blond girl who stood in the middle of the balcony wearing nothing but a bright red bikini, matching heels, and the warm California sun that streamed in through the store's front window.

Now that I've got your attention, it's time for phase two, she silently announced. With a blinding smile, Jessica tossed back her long, loose hair and slowly descended the staircase. Each step had been carefully choreographed to create the greatest impact possible. Just as she'd hoped, every eye in the store remained glued to her—including the very wide, very brown eyes of Bobby Hornet.

As she stepped onto the main floor the crowd's previously awestruck silence gave way to a wave of voices, pointing fingers, and a smattering of applause. Some enterprising store employee had even put on a CD of Handel's "Hallelujah Chorus."

"I can't believe she'd have the nerve!" Tina Chai whispered loudly enough for Jessica to hear.

"Then you don't know Jessica very well," Alexandra Rollins deadpanned.

"Now *that's* a Jessica Wakefield entrance if I ever saw one!" Isabella Ricci said proudly. "Go get 'em, Jess!"

Jessica didn't respond—she was a woman with a mission. She sauntered directly over to Bobby Hornet's table and scooped up the fallen coat, pausing only to take note of Alison Quinn's mortified face.

After she draped the coat casually over her left arm Jessica held out her right hand daintily. "Jessica Wakefield," she said in her breathiest, sultriest voice.

Bobby Hornet continued to sit open-mouthed for a few more seconds before he reached for Jessica's outstretched hand. But just when their fingers were about to touch, Alison sank her claws into Bobby's shoulder, causing his arm to jolt away.

"Bobby, weren't you about to approve *me* for the calendar?"

"Hmmm?" Bobby purred, never taking his eyes off Jessica's.

"*Bob*-by," Alison whined impatiently. "Look at my *pho*-tos." She tapped the pictures laid out in front of him with her finger.

"What? Oh yes, Alice, wasn't it?" Bobby asked distractedly.

"*Aaah-lih-suunn.*"

"OK, OK, Alison."

"Ahem." Jessica shifted her weight to her other foot and threw out a hip, bringing Bobby's full attention back to her. He ran his fingers through his thick, wavy hair, lifting it away from his face.

Alison persisted. "Bobby, you were saying I'd be perfect for the calendar."

"Was I? Maybe. I don't remember, sweetheart. But I can't make my final decision yet. Not until Monday morning."

Bobby brushed Alison away and reached for Jessica's hand, capturing it in his at last. Jessica smiled, holding his gaze as if she had hypnotized him. *Mission accomplished,* she thought, mentally polishing her knuckles in victory. *Game, set, and match.*

"I have decided on one thing, though," Bobby continued. "Jessica Wakefield, I'd like to ask you out. Would you have dinner with me tomorrow night?"

The question hit Jessica unexpectedly, like a Stealth missile. Bobby had followed every step of her plan perfectly until now. He was supposed to promise her the calendar spot, not ask her out.

"Dinner?" she asked innocently, stalling for time. *Go ahead,* a voice inside her urged. *Nick will be on a stakeout tomorrow night anyway. He'll never find out. What's wrong with a little dinner? Besides, if you want to pose for the calendar, you don't have a choice. If you turn Bobby down, you can kiss your chances good-bye.*

Jessica gulped. "Y-Yes, Bobby," she said. "I'd love to have dinner with you tomorrow night."

"What! I *don't* believe it!" Alison shrieked before she turned on her heel and stalked out of the store, leaving her photos behind.

Chapter Six

"No, no, *no!* That's not right at *all!*" Elizabeth growled, staring at her reflection in the mirror. She was going to be meeting Todd in an hour for dinner, and she was trying to find something to wear—something . . . *different.* Elizabeth was hoping that by borrowing something from Jessica's wardrobe, she might lift her spirits and stop worrying about whether or not Gin-Yung Suh—or her mirage—might be lurking around the next corner. But the combination of Jessica's short, beaded cardigan with her own worn-in jeans just wasn't working for her. *Jessica could probably pull this off,* Elizabeth thought morosely. *But not me. Not tonight.*

"Bad idea. Forget it." Elizabeth took off the cardigan and threw it back where she found it— on top of Jessica's messy nightstand, right next to her even messier bed. As she went back to her closet someone knocked at the door.

Elizabeth rolled her eyes and groaned. "Jessica, how could you forget your keys *again?*" she asked out loud. "I'll be there in a minute." She quickly grabbed her SVU sweatshirt from out of her closet and threw it on. Pushing up the sleeves, she walked over to the door and opened it, expecting to find her twin sister preparing yet another lame excuse. But instead she saw her hour-early dinner date.

"Todd!" she exclaimed. "What are you doing here? I thought we were going to meet at the student union."

He ran a hand through his hair brusquely. "I needed to see you sooner. Why don't we go for a walk, Liz."

Elizabeth's heart plummeted to her feet. Todd's brown eyes were deep and serious, and so was his voice. And he wasn't asking her to take a walk with him—he was *telling* her. *Oh no,* she cried silently, feeling her pulse pound a mile a minute. *Please don't let it be true. Please, Todd, don't tell me that it really was Gin-Yung that I saw.*

"Should I . . . ?" Elizabeth tugged at her bulky old sweatshirt to suggest changing out of it.

"No. You look fine."

Hardly, she thought, dejected. *Why won't he let me change? Can't we just put this off for a few more minutes?* But Elizabeth knew it was no use to belabor the point. If the look on his face was any indication, Todd meant business.

"OK," she said reluctantly. Without another word Elizabeth slipped her key into the pocket of her jeans and followed Todd into the hallway. The door shut behind them. The click echoed loudly in Elizabeth's ears, sounding as final as a death sentence.

Neither spoke all the way down the hall or down the stairs. Elizabeth longed to break the silence, but she was too afraid. The quiet tension between them was painful to endure, but Elizabeth knew that whatever Todd had to say would turn out to be much, much worse. And she wanted to put off his telling for as long as possible.

The early evening air felt more stifling than refreshing to Elizabeth when she walked outside. As they headed toward the quad the silence continued. Every once in a while Todd would clear his throat awkwardly and turn to Elizabeth as if to speak. But instead of opening his mouth, he would shake his head slightly and look down at the ground or up at the sky—anywhere but at her face.

Elizabeth decided to follow Todd's example—maybe taking in the scenery would keep her mind occupied. The enormous orange sun rested just above the horizon. The shadows from the trees were long and cool. The scene was incredibly romantic, but the mood was any-thing but.

"How far are we going to walk?" Elizabeth asked at last.

Todd kept charging ahead, his head tucked down, his hands stuffed in his pockets. "I didn't really have anyplace in mind," he replied. "How about the practice fields?"

Elizabeth slowed her pace. She didn't want to walk all the way out to the practice fields. She was tired of walking, and she was tired of wait-ing. Elizabeth couldn't hold out any longer; she wanted—*needed*—to hear what Todd had to say, even though deep down she had a feeling she al-ready knew what it was.

"Why don't we just stop right here," Elizabeth demanded softly, sitting down on the smooth concrete steps of the art building.

Todd obeyed her sheepishly, but he didn't sit. He towered over her on the walkway, ner-vously shifting his weight from one foot to the other.

Elizabeth couldn't take the suspense any longer. She stared up at Todd plainly, openly. "Jin-Yung is back, isn't she?"

"You knew?" Todd took a surprised step backward. "How did you know?"

"I didn't," Elizabeth replied, feeling as if her heart would break. "Not for sure anyway. I thought maybe I saw her yesterday afternoon, but it was only the back of her head. . . . I thought I was seeing things."

Todd sank down onto the step next to her and leaned his chin in his hands. "I thought I was too, Liz. I *wish* I was."

Elizabeth laid a hand on the back of Todd's neck and kissed his shoulder softly. He turned to face her, his eyes wet. His face was so close, Elizabeth could see the little triangular scar over his left eyebrow from his skateboard accident when they were in sixth grade. She reached up and rubbed a finger over the scar gently. Todd closed his eyes. A tear rolled slowly down his cheek.

Please tell me what you're thinking, Todd, she begged silently, but just then he covered his face with his hands. Elizabeth used every ounce of strength she had to pry one of his hands away, grab it, and hold on. And wait.

After a long moment Todd lifted his head and sighed. "Your hand is cold," he said, wrapping both his sturdy hands around hers as if to warm it.

Minutes stretched on. For some reason Elizabeth was reminded of a time when she and Todd were younger and had been on the swim team together. They'd had a contest to see who could hold their breath the longest. Elizabeth felt now the same way she had then; she'd held her breath until she thought she'd die, and then she realized she still had twenty seconds to go to tie Todd's record. She could remember watching the second hand creep around Mr. Wilkins's watch, each second seeming to last an eternity.

Now, as then, she had to breathe—or explode. There didn't seem to be a reason to drag out the agony any longer.

"Todd," she began quietly, hesitantly. "Are we breaking up—again?" She bit her lip to keep it from quivering and gulped back the tears that were threatening to fall.

"No," Todd said hoarsely, urgently. He dropped her hand and draped his arms around her. "Oh no, Liz. That's the last thing I want. We just found each other again. I'm not about to let you go."

"But if Gin-Yung is back—"

"We don't have to go that far."

Again there was a silence that stretched out too long, too painfully.

"What exactly did you bring me out here to say, Todd?"

"I don't really know. I guess . . . I guess I just wanted to let you know about Gin-Yung. I wasn't sure how you'd react." Todd took Elizabeth's hand again and squeezed it firmly, as if to let her know she was handling the news much better than he had expected.

Elizabeth swallowed deliberately. "How did it

feel when you saw her? Did you realize that . . . that you still loved her?"

Todd shook his head. "To be honest, I'm not sure just how I felt. It was too much of a shock. I just didn't expect to see her back so soon. I didn't even get a chance to tell her—"

"About us?"

"No." Todd laughed bitterly. "I'm not handling this very well, am I?"

"Todd, if you don't want to see me anymore—"

"*No*—that's not what I want. I guess I just need a little time. You know, to talk to Gin-Yung—work things out. I still care about her, I guess, but I'm not sure if it's out of obligation or . . ." He trailed off, as if he couldn't bring himself to finish the sentence. "I just don't want to do anything to hurt her."

"Would you rather hurt me again?" Elizabeth asked, almost immediately regretting it.

"No, Liz! It's just that Gin-Yung and I never really broke up—not officially. I'm not sure where we stand. How do *I* know what she thinks?"

"You could ask her." Elizabeth was surprised at the coolness in her own voice.

"I will. I just don't know where to start. And I don't know what I'll do if she—"

"If she's still in love with you?"

"Maybe."

"If she is, Todd, what will you do? Will you go back to her?"

Todd winced, and that one involuntary gesture told Elizabeth everything she didn't want to hear. *Todd still has feelings for Gin-Yung,* she realized. *He may even still love her.* She blinked, and a few tears dropped down onto her SVU sweatshirt.

After a long pause Todd exhaled forcefully. "I just need some time to sort this all out," he said at last. "But it might take a while."

"How long?"

"I don't know, Liz. I just don't know anything right now, except that I love you and I don't want to lose you. Not again."

He dropped his chin onto her shoulder. She could feel the softness of his cheek against hers and the scratchiness of a spot he'd missed while shaving.

"Liz, I guess what I've been trying to say is . . . while I'm getting everything straightened out with Gin-Yung, I have to do it alone. Please don't take this the wrong way, but I don't want her to know that you and I—"

"I understand," she said, pulling away. Her voice was hardly above a whisper. *I understand all too well,* she added silently.

The irony was too painful. Ever since her breakup with Tom Watts, Elizabeth had been pushing Todd away because she needed time alone to straighten out her feelings. But she had chosen Todd in the end, and now that she and Todd were as happy together as they'd ever been, Gin-Yung's inconvenient return was forcing Todd to do the exact same thing to Elizabeth.

Todd looked up at her with tears in his eyes, as if he had at that moment just realized the same thing. "I'm so sorry, Elizabeth. I'll come back to you, I promise."

Maybe you will come back to me, Elizabeth said silently, *and maybe you won't. But one thing I know for sure is that I'm too weak now to try and fight fate.* She'd been through too much these last few weeks. All her strength had been wrung out of her.

Elizabeth swiftly took Todd's face in her hands. His tears were wet against her fingertips. "Don't make me any promises now. Take all the time you need. Talk to Gin-Yung. I won't stand in your way, and I won't ask you to tell her about us. But what I *will* ask you to do is to examine your feelings about Gin-Yung as if—as if we never got back together."

"But how can I—"

"You have to, Todd. Forget these last few weeks completely. It's the only way to be sure that you *really* want to break up with Gin-Yung . . . or

113

if you don't. And if you *do* decide to come back to me, then I'll be waiting for you."

Todd's shoulders began to heave. "Liz, I don't deserve you," he choked out as he wrapped his shaking arms around her. "I really don't. You're too good to me."

"Shhh," Elizabeth murmured, surprised that she was the one comforting him this time. She returned his embrace and held him tightly. "It's OK."

Elizabeth and Todd sat on the stone steps in each other's arms until both their tears subsided. Elizabeth was afraid to let go, wondering if it would be the last time she'd be able to hold Todd, to be this close to him. But in the end she was the first to break away.

"Are you going to be OK?" she asked.

Todd sniffed. "I should be the one asking *you* that."

Elizabeth smiled weakly, glad to see Todd's sense of humor returning. "Don't worry. I have faith in you. I know you'll make the right decision." *Whatever* that *might be,* Elizabeth thought. *I'm not so sure myself. But I can't be selfish. There are more feelings at stake here than my own.*

"Maybe I should let *you* talk to Gin-Yung. You're handling this a lot better than I am."

If you only knew, Elizabeth thought.

Todd got up and stretched, holding out his arms to help Elizabeth to her feet. They stood for a few moments, as if neither one of them wanted to be the first to walk away.

"Well, so much for dinner. My appetite's shot," Todd said as if he were desperate to break the morose mood. "How about you? Are you hungry?"

"No . . . I guess I'd better head back to my dorm."

"I'll walk you."

"*No*, Todd." Elizabeth held out her arms firmly. "Didn't you hear me before? We can't see each other anymore. Not until you've sorted everything out with Gin-Yung."

"But—but I didn't think you really meant—"

"I *did*." Elizabeth could feel her temperature rising. As much as it hurt her to have to put it so plainly, she couldn't think of any other way to say it. "I'll stay out of your way, Todd, if you stay out of mine. We made a deal."

"But I didn't mean—"

Elizabeth put her fingers over Todd's lips. They were soft and warm. How easy it would be to fall into his arms, take back everything she had just said and pretend they were the only two people in the world. But she couldn't do that—not until Todd was sure of what—and who—he really wanted.

"Go talk to Gin-Yung, Todd. I'll accept your decision, whatever it turns out to be." Hastily Elizabeth turned around and hurried down the steps of the art building toward Dickenson Hall. She didn't know how long Todd remained there because she never looked back.

As Elizabeth crossed the quad her knees wobbled a bit and her eyes burned, but she refused to falter. Instead she held her head high, letting the cool night breeze toss her ponytail and her firm resolve guide her steps as she walked to her dorm—alone.

"Come out, come out, wherever you are!" Jessica was rooting around in her closet wildly. "I need a dress that will make Bobby Hornet lose *sleep!*" Like a dog digging for a bone, Jessica was searching for an outfit to wear to her unexpected, and half-unwanted, dinner date tomorrow. She flung piece after piece of unacceptable clothing over one shoulder, covering the entire room with her wardrobe—even Elizabeth's neat-as-a-pin side.

After she'd cleared out her closet, Jessica began rooting around the rest of the room, checking under the bed and even inside her empty wastebasket at one point.

Hearing a key in the door, she gasped. "Elizabeth!" She jumped up and ran to the door. "Oh, Liz, I need *help!*" Jessica wailed as she flung open the door, revealing a much paler and much more dazed-looking version of herself.

Elizabeth said nothing—she didn't even seem to notice the mess. She just walked to her bed and flopped down on it, right on top of a pair of slacks, a purse, and three cotton sweaters.

Oh, well, like this *is anything new,* Jessica thought briefly. *Elizabeth has been such a zombie these days. Maybe Todd Wilkins has turned her into a Stepford girlfriend.* She giggled briefly before launching into her latest trauma.

"Liz, listen. You *have* to help me. I am in the *biggest* jam. I'm freaking out here. I'm going out with *Bobby Hornet* tomorrow night. Well, not exactly *going out,* but . . . oh, I can't lie. I'm going out with him, plain and simple."

Jessica waited for her sister to berate her for supposedly cheating on Nick, but for some bizarre and uncharacteristic reason Elizabeth kept her mouth shut.

"I know it was *the wrong thing to do,*" Jessica said with emphasis, hoping to spur Elizabeth to action. "And I'm feeling *horribly guilty,* but when Bobby asked me out, I *couldn't say no.*"

It didn't seem to work. So Jessica pressed on, if not for Elizabeth's benefit, then for her own. "If I turned him down, I probably wouldn't get picked to be in that bikini calendar I told you about. And Nick really wants me to be in the calendar. So if he wants me to be in it *that* bad, then I guess he wouldn't mind if I had a little

117

dinner with one of the most popular and gorgeous singers in America, right? I guess, in a way, I'm doing this for Nick."

Silence.

"Oh—forget it. I can't keep making excuses. But the guilt is eating me alive! How can I go through with this? I love Nick so much, and I don't want to do anything to lose him. If he found out about my dinner date tomorrow, he would go ballistic. But if I *don't* go out with Bobby Hornet, then I won't get in the calendar. And then what will happen? Nick wouldn't be able to show me off, and then I might not have a career after I graduate, and . . . *jeez*, Lizzie, what is *wrong* with you?"

Jessica put her hands on her hips and looked at her twin sideways. "Is this some new psychology technique you're trying out on me? Because if it is, it's not working. It's only making me crazier. Quit trying to ignore me. I'll clean up this mess later, I promise."

Elizabeth continued to stare at the ceiling.

Jessica cupped her hands like a megaphone. "Elizabeth Wakefield! *Can you hear me?*" she shouted. "Have you heard a single word I've said?"

Elizabeth rolled over and faced the wall.

"*Li-i-i-i-z*, what should I *dooooo?*"

Suddenly Elizabeth burst into tears. She didn't simply start crying; tears exploded out of her like

118

lava from a volcano. Jessica jumped back in fear.

Elizabeth pounded her bed with her fist. "It doesn't matter *what* you do," she sobbed with full force. "Because there's no such thing as love anyway. It *never* works out. It's always a horrible, stupid tragedy." Angrily she shoved Jessica's things off her bed, flopped over onto her stomach, and buried her face in her pillow. She sobbed as if she would never stop.

Is it something I said? Jessica wondered. This burst of emotion was unlike any that Jessica had ever seen from her sister. It almost scared her.

Jessica sat down tentatively on Elizabeth's bed. "Liz, I'm sorry if I got on your nerves."

Elizabeth wailed even more loudly.

"I should have known you were upset when you came in the door. I'm sorry I didn't pay any attention. Please talk to me. Please tell me what happened."

Her sister's sobs seemed to die down, but she still wouldn't budge or speak. Jessica tried to imagine what Elizabeth would do if the situation were reversed. How would Elizabeth get her to talk if she was stoked up like a pressure cooker ready to blow?

"Is—is it Tom?" Jessica asked hesitantly, gasping when Elizabeth suddenly bolted up in place, her eyes no longer sad or pained but fiercely angry.

"*No!* No, it's *not* Tom! I'm sick and tired of people thinking I'm all broken up over *Tom!*"

"OK! OK!" There seemed to be only one other option. "Was it Todd, then?

Elizabeth sniffed loudly.

Gotcha, Jessica thought. "All right. What did Todd do now?"

"*Nothing.*"

Jessica raised an eyebrow. "Now, he must have done something. It's nothing like when you guys broke up before, is it? Did he try to force himself on you?"

"No, it's not that at all. He—he just—"

"He *what?* Tell me now, Liz, or I'm going to track him down and throw him to the Thetas."

Elizabeth didn't laugh, but a tiny smile crossed her face. "It's not Todd—not really. Gin-Yung is back."

"No! He's not going back to her, is he?"

"I don't know yet." Elizabeth sniffed, her voice becoming cool and unemotional, just like it had when she was back on the steps with Todd. "He just told me that he needs time to sort things out—alone. He has to talk things over with Gin-Yung and find out . . . and find out if he should choose her . . . or me."

"That's no contest, Liz, and you know it. Todd would be crazy to let you go again."

"But I put him up to it, Jess!" Elizabeth

exclaimed. "I told him that we shouldn't see each other anymore until he got it all sorted out. And I more or less told him that I didn't want to be with him if he had any feelings left for Gin-Yung at all."

"Does he?"

"I *know* he does—I can just tell." Elizabeth put her head in her hands and wept. "If I lose Todd again, it'll be all my fault. I think I made a big mistake."

Jessica hugged her sister until she was all cried out. "Everything's going to be fine, Liz, you'll see," she said, stroking her hair. "Todd will come back. Like I said, he'd be crazy not to."

"I hope you're right," Elizabeth said, pulling away and rubbing her weary, reddened eyes.

"Look, Liz, why don't you go take a long hot shower, and I'll make us some tea." Jessica was shocked to hear those words coming from her lips—she must have heard Elizabeth make that same suggestion to her hundreds of times. But when Elizabeth managed a weak smile, Jessica knew she'd said the right thing. "Then we'll both hit the sack. You'll feel better tomorrow."

"OK." She sniffed. "Thanks for listening, Jess."

"Hey, what are sisters for, right?"

Jessica watched her sister with pride as she gathered up her things and headed out to the shower room. Elizabeth had frightened her with her outburst—and somehow, in some way, Jessica had been able to cheer her up. "I guess that's my good deed for the day," she said out loud, but deep down she knew it was far more than that. Before she got a chance to ponder it further, she noticed her red bikini, which had been flung haphazardly over the computer monitor.

"Ugghh." Jessica covered her eyes. "Guilt, guilt, go away!" She turned away from the incriminating bikini and looked out the window. The fluorescent lights outside flickered and blinked, and suddenly Jessica caught a glimpse of a flash among the bushes—as if the light was reflected on a camera lens, or maybe a pair of binoculars.

Flinging open the window, Jessica stuck her head outside. "Who's there?" she demanded, hardly believing her eyes when she saw the bushes move as if someone were scurrying through them.

"Jerk!" Jessica hollered before slamming the window back down. "Some prank," she reasoned aloud. "Some stupid frat boy spying on the girls' dorm. What a loser!"

Or maybe it was Nick. She froze at the idea. Even though it seemed awfully far-fetched, Jessica still dashed over to the computer, grabbed the red bikini, and stuffed it away in a desk drawer. *Evidence!* she thought. *I have to hide the evidence!*

Jessica ran back to the window—no sign of

anyone. Not a living thing. She continued to look outside, wondering where Nick was and what he was doing at that moment. *Maybe he's thinking about me,* Jessica thought, and smiled. But her smile faded when she realized that whatever her gorgeous, perfect, and *faithful* boyfriend was doing, saying, or thinking, he was completely and utterly clueless to the fact that Jessica was about to go on a date with another guy.

As guilt came washing back over her like a tidal wave Jessica closed her eyes. "Oh, Nick," she whispered against the windowpane. "Nick, I hope you can forgive me."

It was nearly midnight when Tom parked his car in front of Dana's house. They had been together ever since their brunch at the Seacliff Inn—over fourteen hours—and still he couldn't believe how quickly the time had passed. He was reluctant to let her go even now.

"This day has been amazing," Tom said, looking over at Dana. Her hair had come down from the semiorderly French twist she'd worn at breakfast and was now loose around her face in a halo of dark curls.

"I know."

"Every minute—every *hour*—we spent together—fantastic! I mean, I can't remember the last time I went to the zoo."

"Me either!" Dana reached up and ran a tickling finger across his lips. "I loved the brunch and the flowers." She giggled. "*And* the champagne."

"And the movie?"

"I don't remember a movie," Dana said teasingly.

"That's because you weren't paying *attention*. We were too busy . . ." Tom leaned over and gave Dana a long, lingering kiss.

"Oh, *that* movie!" Dana cooed when they came up for air. "I remember now. I'm surprised we didn't get thrown out."

Laughing heartily, Tom gave her a peck on the cheek for good measure. "Look, I'd really like to see you tomorrow, but I'm already meeting George and the kids for dinner."

"Tell them I said hi, OK?"

Tom smiled, glad that Dana understood how much spending time with his new family meant to him. She'd never ask him to change his plans for her. Dana wasn't jealous of the Conroys—not like that other girl he used to know.

"How about Sunday?" he suggested. "I can borrow George's convertible. We'll take a long drive up the coast."

"Well . . . I don't know," she teased. "I've just *got* to cram for biology."

"Why don't you bring your books? We can study. Or something."

"OK. It's a date." Dana opened her arms and drew Tom's face toward her own. Tom was so completely lost in her kiss, he forgot where he was until his elbow slipped and hit the car horn.

"*Shhh*. You'll wake the whole neighborhood." Dana giggled mischievously and scooted away.

"Come back here. I'll be quiet."

"If I do, I might never leave. I really should go inside, Tom. It's getting late."

"I'll walk you to the door."

Dana shook her head. "No, don't bother." She reached into the backseat and gathered up the yellow roses he'd given her at brunch. They were slightly crushed and rather droopy now, but Dana cradled them lovingly in her arms.

"Now go do your homework," Tom said firmly, "and I'll call you tomorrow to make sure we're still on."

"OK. 'Night, Tom." She closed the car door with a flick of her hips and blew him a kiss through the open window.

Tom leaned back against the headrest and watched her run up the sidewalk to the porch. He wouldn't leave until he knew she was safely inside. When he saw the light come on in what he supposed was her bedroom, he started the car.

When he glanced into the rearview mirror as he pulled away from the curb, Tom was startled by his own reflection. *I'm smiling*, he thought. *I haven't seen myself smile for a long, long time.*

Tom turned on the radio and began tapping his fingers on the steering wheel in time to the music. It seemed as if the dark clouds hanging over his life had finally broken.

Yes, he thought. *If anyone on this planet can make me forget Miss Elizabeth Wakefield, it's Dana Upshaw.*

Chapter Seven

Might as well face it, Jessica thought as she hurried across the quad toward Theta house. *If this guilt keeps driving me crazy, I'll have to be shipped off to the funny farm.* Her only hope of sanity was to surround herself with the security of the Thetas. Maybe a Saturday afternoon of gossip, coffee, and sisterhood would get her mind off her date with Bobby Hornet that night.

But as she darted past the campus coffee shop she stopped in her tracks when she saw Gin-Yung Suh and her older sister coming out, cups in hand.

Jessica gulped, suddenly remembering Elizabeth's crying fit the night before. Her dilemma seemed awfully petty in comparison to Elizabeth's. Here she'd just gotten back together with Todd, and now who knew what would happen? And it was all because Gin-Yung had to come back and spoil everything. Jessica wasn't about to sit back and watch her sister's heart get broken—not again.

I did one good deed for Liz last night, Jessica thought as she narrowed her eyes and pushed up her sleeves. *Now it's time for good deed number two.*

Gin-Yung and her sister disappeared into Waggoner Hall, and Jessica took off after them. "This one's for you, Liz," she murmured as she threw open Waggoner Hall's heavy front doors.

Jessica spotted Gin-Yung and her sister standing by one of the staff offices along the near corridor. She walked past them as if she was there on her own business, suddenly stopping right in front of them with feigned surprise. "Gin-Yung! You're back!" she cried mock excitedly, her voice echoing in the empty, high-ceilinged hallways.

"How are you . . ." Gin-Yung trailed off and tilted her head to one side. Jessica recognized the look immediately—she'd seen it all her life. Gin-Yung was trying to figure out which Wakefield twin she was talking to.

"Jessica," she prompted.

Gin-Yung smiled. "Of course, Jessica. I knew it was you."

"Sure. Weren't you just in Ireland or Kenya or something?"

"London."

"*Right*, London," Jessica said with an insignificant flick of her wrist. "So, what brings you back to campus? Just visiting?"

"I'm returning a few books that Professor Keene loaned to me."

"Oh. You must be heading back to London now, I take it."

Gin-Yung's smile wilted. "No, actually. I'm back. For good."

"Oh! That's right. I knew that. Well, I guess you've already heard the news, then."

"What news?" Gin-Yung gasped, bringing a hand to her throat. She looked positively terrified.

"Uh, Gin?" Kim put a protective hand on Gin-Yung's arm. "Maybe we should come back later."

"No, Kim, I want to hear. What news?"

Jessica smiled conspiratorially. "Didn't you hear that Todd Wilkins and my sister aren't seeing each other anymore?"

Gin-Yung turned pale, and her chest seemed to collapse right before Jessica's eyes. "I—I don't know what you mean. Todd and Elizabeth broke up a long time ago."

"Oh, I don't mean *that*. I mean last night. They'd gotten back together while you were away, Gin-Yung. Didn't you hear?"

"No," Gin-Yung whispered. "No, I didn't."

"Really? That's surprising. Because I *distinctly*

129

heard that the reason Todd and Elizabeth stopped dating is because—now, let me get this straight—because *Todd* felt that he might have an obligation to get back together with *you*." Jessica raised an eyebrow. "Funny that you'd be the last to know."

Gin-Yung said nothing. She slumped against Kim, who was giving Jessica the most evil eye she'd ever seen.

"Oh, well, I guess that's the way it goes sometimes," Jessica finished brightly. "Ta-ta."

Her work done, Jessica twirled on her sandaled heel and flounced away. When she burst through the doors into the sunny afternoon, she smiled. No wonder Elizabeth was always doing good deeds for people. It felt *great*.

But before Theta house even came into view, Jessica remembered that her date with Bobby Hornet was coming up—*fast*—and the good feeling whooshed out of her like air out of a balloon. Suddenly a vision of Nick's face appeared before her. In her mind's eye his expression turned from sweetly sexy to darkly disappointed—a transition she hated to see.

Oh, please help me, somebody, she silently pleaded. *I've done so many nice things lately. Help me get through this night before I have a nervous breakdown!*

* * *

Gin-Yung sank down against the wall as she watched Jessica fly out the front doors of Waggoner Hall. The doors slammed resoundingly, the loud echo giving way to deafening silence.

Kim bent down and put a protective arm around her sister's shoulders. "Don't pay any attention to her," she demanded. "You know Jessica. She's living proof that human life-forms evolved from primordial ooze."

"No, Kim, you're wrong," Gin-Yung said, her voice barely above a whisper. "Don't you get it? That's why Todd was being so distant on the phone—that's why he was so shocked to see me. He must have been seeing Elizabeth again. I don't want to believe it, but . . . but there's just no other explanation."

"Don't be silly. I know just as well as you do that Elizabeth and Todd have been friends since they were in diapers. Just because they've been hanging around together doesn't mean they're 'together'—you know what I mean?"

"But Jessica said—"

"From what I've heard, Jessica Wakefield is famous for speaking before thinking."

"I could never compete with Elizabeth," Gin-Yung said bleakly. "Not if he wants her back."

"That's ridiculous."

"No, it isn't. You don't know Todd like I do,

Kim. I know how much Todd loved her."

"*Loved*—that's past tense, Gin-Yung. *You're* Todd's girlfriend now. Don't you think he would have said something to you?"

Gin-Yung sadly shook her head. She knew all too well that Elizabeth was the only person who had the power to come between her and Todd. Yet at the same time she was the last person Gin-Yung expected to do it.

When she left for London, Elizabeth and Tom Watts were inseparable. Todd would have told her if they had broken up . . . wouldn't he?

"But think of what Jessica said," Gin-Yung began shakily. "She said that Todd was going to come back to me out of *obligation*. That's just like him. He hurt Elizabeth so badly when they broke up the first time—he never really got over it. He became terrified of ever hurting anyone again. He *wouldn't* tell me if he'd gotten back together with Elizabeth, Kim. He's too afraid to."

Tears welled up in Gin-Yung's eyes when she realized what she'd said. She'd just convinced herself that the last thing in the world she wanted to believe might actually be true.

"What you *don't* need right now," Kim said, "is to drive yourself crazy by justifying these horrible lies."

But it's all true, Gin-Yung replied silently. And

as much as she loved Todd, she couldn't keep him from living his life the way he wanted to.

"Think about what you want, Gin-Yung. Be selfish for a change."

Gin-Yung turned her tearstained face to look squarely at her sister. "I want Todd to be happy," she said softly. "That's what I want."

"*You* make him happy."

"Maybe I don't, Kim. I don't own him. Todd is capable of making his own choices. If he's happy with Elizabeth, then who am I to interfere?"

"You're Todd's *girlfriend,* that's who!"

"I *was* his girlfriend."

"Stop it," Kim demanded. "Please. You're forgetting that Todd's coming over tonight. Why would he do that if he was back with Elizabeth?"

"He's not, remember? He broke up with her again because he has an obligation—"

"Lies!" Kim put her hands to her head as if she wanted to rip her own hair out in frustration. "All lies. You'll talk to Todd tonight, Gin. He'll prove it all wrong."

More than anything Gin-Yung wanted to believe her sister. But there was no way she could—the evidence was too strong.

"Your own happiness is at stake here," Kim said, her voice soft and caring. "You're scared, I know. And it's going to be hard for you to tell Todd what you have to say. But whatever happens

133

tonight—just try and make the most of it. For your sake."

Happiness. Gin-Yung sighed long and hard. *What does it matter anyway.* If Todd wanted to be with Elizabeth, he'd probably be better off. How could her own happiness compare with theirs? It couldn't—hers was futile, a waste. *It wouldn't be fair for me to take Todd away from Elizabeth now,* she realized coldly. *Not when I would just be leaving him again.*

Gin-Yung's tears turned into heaving sobs. She wished she'd never left Sweet Valley University . . . never taken that pointless internship in London. Never gone to that stupid, stupid doctor.

"Oh, Gin . . . please don't," Kim said tearfully, putting both her arms around her sister and holding her. "Let's get away from this campus, OK? And when we get home, you're going to take a long hot bubble bath, and then I'll let you wear anything in my closet. We'll get ready for Todd together, all right?"

Wiping her face on her sleeve, Gin-Yung sniffed and managed a weak nod. Kim jumped to her feet and helped Gin-Yung up off the floor, and when she offered Gin-Yung a pair of sunglasses to hide her tear-reddened eyes, she gratefully took them. But as she put them on she shivered with fear. She knew what she had to do tonight, and a bubble bath and a new outfit weren't going to make it any easier.

Even though it was past noon, Elizabeth still hadn't gotten out of bed. She'd been awake most of the morning, but she couldn't muster up the energy to actually get up. Sunlight streamed in around the edges of the window shade, but the room was still mostly dark.

To keep her mind off the events of last night, Elizabeth was concentrating on the goofy glow-in-the-dark star stickers that Jessica had stuck all over the ceiling. Almost as if her stare was as destructive as her mood, a star suddenly came loose, falling into a pile of junk on Jessica's bed, never to be seen again.

Shooting stars—that reminded Elizabeth of something. Who was just talking about shooting stars? Nina. *That's who I need right now,* she realized. *I need to talk to Nina.* And since it was a Saturday afternoon, she knew exactly where she could find her.

With a sudden burst of adrenaline Elizabeth rolled out of bed and grabbed a pair of jeans. She noticed that her navy long-sleeved T-shirt was hanging over her lampshade. *So much for Jessica's promise to clean up her mess,* she thought dryly as she picked up the shirt and put it on. After she brushed her teeth, washed her face, and threw her hair back in a ponytail, she grabbed her book bag and headed for the library.

Elizabeth got there in a flash. She hurried up the steps to the second floor, and there she found Nina in her usual carrel, studying away furiously, just like she'd expected.

"Hey," Elizabeth whispered as she walked to the carrel across from Nina's—her usual studying space. She and Nina had logged in so many hours in those carrels that the librarian often teased them by saying she'd be billing them for rent at the end of the year.

Nina glanced up and smiled, and Elizabeth motioned for Nina to keep working. Her story could be put off until Nina's next study break. Besides, it wouldn't hurt for her to get some studying done herself—it'd take her mind off things. She pulled her heavy English lit book from her bag and turned to the section on Alfred, Lord Tennyson.

Elizabeth loved poetry, but as she continued to read Tennyson she found herself getting more and more depressed. "In Memoriam" seemed to drag on and on. It was all a blur until she got to stanza 27. Two lines practically jumped off the page at her: "'Tis better to have loved and lost / Than never to have loved at all."

She slammed the heavy book shut with a thud. Those had to have been the two worst lines ever written in the English language! Tennyson evidently had *no* idea what it felt like to love someone as much as she loved Todd. She'd lost him once before and now—*maybe*—she was about to lose him again. It was the worst feeling she'd ever known. Would the pain be even worse the second time around?

Elizabeth winced as her eyes began to sting. *Tennyson was* wrong, she thought. *I'd be much better off if I'd never, ever, fallen in love. At least I wouldn't keep getting hurt.*

Against her will Elizabeth played over both her breakups in her mind. First Todd—devastating. Then Tom—horrible. And now Todd again—if it really happened, it would be the worst of all. Because she knew just how much Todd loved her. And while she'd be all alone, Tom would have Dana—and Todd would have Gin-Yung.

Love isn't worth the pain, she realized as a tear slowly trickled down her cheek and landed on the textbook, right on the word *never.* She shoved the book aside, laid her head in the crook of her arm, and started to sob.

If she'd learned anything in college this year, it was how to cry silently. And she did. She cried and cried as if her heart were breaking, but she still hadn't mastered the skill of silent sniffling. Nothing she tried had ever been able to control that horrible reflex that came after crying too long; when all the air in the room wasn't enough, and she couldn't seem to breathe anymore without a struggle. She wrapped her arms more tightly around her head in an attempt to muffle the sound of her sniffling.

But it didn't work. Someone tapped her shoulder. She glanced up to see a Kleenex dangling inches from her face. Gratefully she took it, and Nina scooted up a chair beside her.

"OK, Liz. Tell the future psychiatrist all about it."

"You aren't a future psychiatrist," Elizabeth said, pausing to blow her nose. "You're a future physicist."

"Well, what difference do a few letters make? Anyway, with all the counseling practice I've been getting lately, I might as well change my major."

"I'm sorry. It seems like all I've been doing lately is unloading my problems on you."

Nina held out her arm. "Hold it right there. There's no need to apologize. My ears are yours. Let's have it."

Elizabeth took a deep breath. "Oh, Nina," she cried. "Why does every guy I love end up leaving me? First Tom breaks up with me and finds Dana, and then Todd—"

"Whoa, whoa, back up the train," Nina demanded, waving her hands excitedly. "What's all this about Tom all of a sudden? You've already worked through that thing, remember? Don't tell me you're blaming yourself for the breakup again. Because you know that was all his fault."

"I know, but he's found someone else—Dana, the girl he was with at the poetry reading. He's got someone now, and I don't."

Nina tilted her head to the side and scrunched up her face quizzically. "Wait a minute, Liz. Am I missing something here? Since when do you *not* have anyone?"

"Since last night, Nina." Elizabeth scribbled aimlessly on the cover of her notebook, trying to fight back the tears that were threatening to spill again. "That's what I came here to tell you about. Gin-Yung came back."

"*What?* For good?"

"I think so. And Todd's thinking about going back to her. He's going to break up with me again, Nina, I just know it."

Elizabeth began to sob, not only because of Todd but because she was dreading Nina's response. She'd warned Elizabeth about getting back together with Todd when she was still on the rebound from Tom. Nina had told her to go slow and easy, but Elizabeth hadn't taken her advice.

Elizabeth watched her best friend anxiously as she cracked her knuckles, a habit of Nina's that usually indicated she was holding back. But instead of Nina's passing any judgments, Elizabeth was thankful when Nina simply cleared her throat and asked her to explain everything from the beginning. True friend that Nina was, she didn't even say, "I told you so." And after Elizabeth was finished, Nina gave her a comforting hug.

"I think you did the right thing," Nina said, patting her on the back. "Give Todd some time to let him get his head together before he comes back to you."

"But what if he *doesn't* come back to me?"

Nina dug a fresh tissue out of her book bag and passed it over. "It'll be all right, Liz. Even though I didn't know you guys when you were dating back in high school, I can tell you were made for each other."

"*Were,* maybe, but not anymore."

Nina let out an exasperated groan. "Come on, now. Todd didn't say he didn't love you. He didn't even say he wanted to break up with you. You're the one who said that."

"But I know he's going to have to get together with her. I don't have any problem with Gin-Yung personally, and I know I shouldn't feel this way. But just the thought of them together drives me crazy. I want him to be happy, but—"

"I think you're getting ahead of yourself," Nina interrupted. "Didn't you say he needed time to resolve the thing with Gin-Yung?"

"Yes, but—"

"Then how do you know he's not breaking up with her right now? Everyone knows how much Todd loves you. When you think about it, Gin-Yung was just a transitional phase—between you and you. Have some faith in him."

Elizabeth desperately needed to hear Nina's comforting words, but no matter how much she wanted to believe them, she couldn't convince herself to. It was like running cold water over a burn: It helped for a second, but when it was over, the pain came right back again.

"You just need to quit feeling sorry for yourself, Liz. And even if—God forbid—Todd does go back to Gin-Yung, since when do you need a man to make you happy? You're beautiful, brilliant, and have great friends like me."

"But—"

"But nothing. You can concentrate on your work at WSVU. I'll bet when Tom graduates, you'll be running that place, if not before."

"I can't even set foot in there. When I bumped into Tom the other day, I ran out like an idiot."

"OK, so you put the station on hold. So what? You still have your classes to think about. You can't let your grades fall off just because some guy is giving you a hard way to go. Guys aren't everything."

"Easy for you to say. You have Bryan." But

Elizabeth knew, even as she said it, she wasn't being entirely fair. Nina made it clear Bryan wasn't her only reason for living. She could be a complete, successful person with or without a man.

Even though everything Nina had said made perfect sense, it still didn't seem like enough. It didn't stop the gnawing feeling in the pit of her stomach or the dull ache in her chest. Maybe nobody could understand what she was feeling— not even her best friend. Maybe nobody had ever loved anyone as much as she loved Todd.

Am I the only person who ever felt this way? Elizabeth wondered as a new wave of tears overwhelmed her. *I can't be alone . . . no, I just can't. Someone has to understand me or I'll lose my mind. I don't think I can handle being this lonely—alone.*

Chapter
Eight

I hope she's called, Tom thought as he let himself into his dorm room. He tossed his books onto his bed and dropped a stack of tape cases onto the floor beside his VCR. He'd been at WSVU all morning, catching up on work—he couldn't believe that he'd let it pile up so badly.

Stretching out across the bed, he tapped the play button on his answering machine. The first message was from Professor Sedder, head of the communications department, who was checking up on a story Tom was supposed to have been preparing. "I got your message at the station," Tom said impatiently as the professor's taped voice droned on and on. "I'm working on it, already."

The next message was from a guy named Scott who'd dropped off some of his press clips at the station in the hopes of doing an internship. "I'm reading 'em, I'm reading 'em," Tom assured the answering machine.

The third and last call was from Brett Ryder, who invited him to another frat party. "Forget it," he growled, sinking back on the bed, disappointed. He wanted so much to hear Dana's voice. Why hadn't she called? He figured that the least she could do was check in and say hi. Maybe Dana hadn't had as much fun as he did on Friday. Maybe she didn't want to see him on Sunday. Well, there was only one way to find out. He *had* said he'd be the one to call her, after all.

Nervously he picked up the phone and dialed. A busy signal buzzed in his ear. *How could anybody* not *have call waiting?* Tom wondered as he slammed down the phone. Ignoring the jittery feeling in his torso, he reached in his backpack for the press clips, figuring he could get a little work done while he waited for her line to clear.

At least it was quiet for once. Usually Rod, the guy in the room next door, felt the need to share his music with the entire dorm. And if Rod wasn't shaking the rafters with his supercharged stereo system, the guys in the room upstairs were dribbling a basketball or playing what Tom called the throw-a-bowling-ball-into-the-trash-can-right-over-Tom's-desk game.

Dorm life could really be a pain sometimes.

He piled his pillows in a corner of the bed

and kicked off his shoes, hoping to get comfortable. But that was impossible with the phone sitting right there, taunting him. He picked up the receiver and tried again. Still busy.

He sank back onto the pillows and flipped through the clips. They didn't look half bad. Tom was almost enjoying himself when Rod's stereo suddenly roared to life. The walls started to vibrate to the rhythm of rap.

Tom threw the clips aside and banged on the wall, but it didn't seem to make a difference. The pounding of the music and the pounding of his fist seemed to be one and the same. *You just can't get any work done in this place,* he told himself, barely able to hear his own thoughts. *I give up.*

Angrily Tom tried calling Dana a third time, but he still couldn't get through. To add to his mounting frustration, a framed news-reporting award came loose from the wall and smashed somewhere behind the VCR.

"That does it!" Tom shouted aloud. "I'm outta here." He put on his shoes and slung his backpack over his shoulder. Since he was going to Los Angeles to have supper with the Conroys anyway, he'd just show up a little earlier than planned. He could call Dana when he got there and besides could spend the extra time working—and relaxing—in his father's quiet, luxurious condo.

The music paused for a moment, and Tom

groaned with relief. But the precious silence was punctuated by the slam of a door. Tom jumped, looking up to see that his roommate, Danny Wyatt, had just walked in.

"Hey, stranger," Danny said good-naturedly. "Long time, no see. Or maybe you don't remember me. I live here."

"Very funny," Tom snarled as the music started up again.

"What's got you in such a charming mood?" Danny hollered.

"This place is impossible! How is anyone supposed to study with that racket?"

"Never fails, does it?" Danny yelled as he peeled off his jeans. "The minute we get back to our room, it's time for the daily concert."

"Like clockwork," Tom agreed. "I think he has radar."

Danny stepped into a pair of SVU sweats. "Well, let him play. I'm going for a jog. You wanna come?"

"No, thanks. I think I'm going to head over to George's a little early. Get some work done."

"C'mon, Tombo. We haven't gone running together for ages. Running alone is a drag."

"You go sweat. I'm heading for L.A."

Danny raised an eyebrow. "You've been spending an awful lot of time with the Conroys these days."

"Why shouldn't I? They're my family now," Tom snapped.

"Hey, don't get bent out of shape."

"Sorry, man. Actually I'm not spending *all* my time with the Conroys." Tom gave his roommate a sly grin.

"Oh, I get it. Does this have something to do with the tiny, dark-haired beauty that Izzy and I saw you with last week?"

Tom nodded. "You got it. Her name's Dana."

"Yeah, Dana. I remember. How's it going with you two?"

"Couldn't be better," Tom said confidently, despite his worries to the contrary. "She's pretty wild, but she's sweet too. I think you'd like her."

"Good for you, Tombo." Danny clapped him on the back. "Hey, did you notice something?"

Tom paused for a moment. "No, what?"

Danny laughed. "Maybe it's what you *didn't* notice. I think our daily serenade is over."

For a long moment Tom and Danny stood in silence and listened. The music seemed to have stopped.

"Great," Tom said, throwing down his backpack. "I've gotta make one last call before I go." He dove for the phone and dialed. *Yes*—it rang!

After about five rings it picked up. "Hello?" came a sleepy, unfamiliar female voice. *Must be one of Dana's roommates,* Tom reasoned.

"Hi, is Dana there?"

"Who's calling?"

Tom was surprised he was being asked that. "Tom Watts," he replied, unnerved.

"I don't know if she's here. Let me find out."

Tom heard a clunking sound, as if the receiver on the other end had been dropped. *Maybe Dana asked her roommates to screen her calls,* he thought, his heart pounding. *Maybe she's trying to avoid me.* He could feel Danny's eyes on him, watching him closely. A burning sensation came over Tom's face. He didn't want his roommate to see him get shot down.

Come on, Dana, pick up the phone, Tom begged silently. He desperately hoped that Dana still wanted to go out with him. Because if she didn't, it would mean that Elizabeth Wakefield had won.

Tom sank onto his bed, phone in hand. *Where did* that *thought come from?* he wondered. *Elizabeth would have won* what? Elizabeth had nothing to do with him and Dana—or did she? Was he pushing his relationship with Dana only to prove to Elizabeth that he could replace her as easily as she'd replaced him? If Dana didn't want him, would that make him a failure?

Yes, it would, Tom realized with a scowl. *Because she'd still have Wilkins. And meanwhile I'd have . . . nobody.*

"Hello? Is anyone there?"

"Dana!" Tom switched the receiver to his other hand and wiped a sweaty hand on his jeans.

"Tom, how are you?"

"I'm fine," he said, but he didn't feel fine. He felt as wound up as a bad watch. He would be devastated if she didn't want to see him tomorrow.

"I'm so glad you called. I was going to call you earlier, but I've just been so busy."

Tom breathed a sigh of relief. "I'm glad to hear that," he said, looking over to shoot Danny a triumphant smile. But Danny had already left.

"So, Tom, do you still want to get together tomorrow? I know I do."

Tom blinked. It was too good to be true. *Dana* was asking *him* if they were still on!

"Absolutely."

"Great. I should finish my bio assignment tonight. Maybe I can even get in a little cello practice. Then I'll be all yours."

Perfect. "How does one sound?"

"Sounds good, Tom. I can't wait."

"Me either."

After they said their good-byes, Tom hung up and yelled, "Yes!" He couldn't have been more psyched. As he picked up his backpack again his chest swelled with pride. Not just because Dana wanted to see him tomorrow, but because he really and truly *cared* that Dana wanted to see him tomorrow.

Maybe I am *actually falling in love again,* Tom thought as he soared out the door. *That was almost too easy!*

Why isn't love ever easy? Todd thought as he stood on the porch outside Gin-Yung's parents' house. Dread hung over him like a cloud. He felt like a little kid being called to the principal's office.

Both Winston and Elizabeth had convinced him of what he already knew: He needed to have a heart-to-heart with Gin-Yung. Still, he'd probably have put if off another day or two if Gin-Yung hadn't called and asked him to come over.

Even now he had no idea of what he was going to say, exactly. He just hoped he'd be able to stay composed and sound convincing—not just stand there and stammer like he'd done when she'd surprised him at his dorm room.

Right when he pushed the doorbell again, Gin-Yung's sister Kim flung open the door. The look she gave him made him feel more nervous than he already was. Motioning for him to come inside, she slammed the door behind her with more force than Todd thought was necessary.

"You're late," she said.

"Am I?" Todd knew he was late, but he didn't think it was any of Kim's business. "Sorry." He followed Kim into the living room.

"Sit down," Kim ordered, pointing at a couch. "Gin-Yung will be down in just a few minutes."

"That's OK. There's no rush." Todd sank onto the couch and scrunched his long legs into the space between the couch and the coffee table. Kim remained standing.

"So," Kim began, crossing her arms in front of her. "Gin tells me you're back on the basketball team."

"Yes. Practice keeps me pretty busy."

"I guess that explains things."

"Excuse me?" Todd asked, surprised.

Kim said nothing.

"Are you trying to say that I didn't come see Gin-Yung soon enough? I didn't even know she was back until yesterday morning."

"Relax, Todd. I was just making conversation."

Maybe so, but I wish you'd quit making it with that suspicious look on your face, Todd thought. He picked up a sports magazine from the coffee table and began to thumb through it anxiously, hoping Kim would just go away. But Kim stood there, making him incredibly uncomfortable.

Todd decided to take one more stab at polite conversation. "Wow, this magazine is from England," he said lamely. "I guess Gin-Yung brought home a lot of souvenirs."

"I guess so."

Todd blinked in amazement. Everything Kim

151

said and did seemed to have several different layers of meaning. He'd never had trouble getting along with her before. Surely she didn't suspect— *No,* he thought. *There's no way she could possibly know about me and Elizabeth.*

"Gin really missed you while she was away," Kim said in a slightly softer tone.

"I missed her too," he said automatically, afraid to say anything more. He was relieved when he finally heard Gin-Yung coming down the stairs.

Kim came over and leaned close to Todd's ear. "Our parents are out," she whispered tartly. "But I'll be right next door in the kitchen."

Todd gaped at Kim's retreating figure. What was *that* supposed to mean? It sounded almost like a warning or a threat. Did she think he was going to pounce on Gin-Yung the second he got her alone?

"Hi, Todd," Gin-Yung said quietly.

"Hey, Gin." Todd jumped up, but she motioned for him to sit back down.

Although there was plenty of room beside him on the sofa, Gin-Yung chose to sit across from him in the big recliner.

For the first time since Gin-Yung's return, Todd took a long look at her. She looked different—a *lot* different. He guessed it was because the loafers, khaki pants, and white cotton shirt she usually wore had been replaced by a deep red, one-piece pantsuit that seemed far too big and baggy on her.

"I like your, uh—outfit." He never could remember the proper names for women's clothes.

"Thanks, but it's Kim's. She wanted me to dress up like a girl tonight."

"You always look like a girl, Gin-Yung, no matter *what* you're wearing. Is that what was taking you so long? I was about to come upstairs and get you."

"I'm sorry I kept you waiting."

"No, that's OK. It's just"—he lowered his voice—"your sister. She was acting a little strange. Is she upset about something?"

"Kim? Who knows. I'm not sure just how she feels half the time." Gin-Yung's face turned a bit wistful, and an uncomfortable silence fell over the room.

"Well," Todd began, not sure of what to say next. "How's Chung-Hee? She's seven, right?"

Gin-Yung's face brightened immediately at the mention of her little sister's name. "Right. She's fine, as sweet as ever. She had a dance recital tonight. That's where my parents are right now."

"Didn't you want to go?"

"Sure, but . . . those things always make me a little crazy. They seem to go on forever. Besides, I really wanted to see you."

Todd cast his eyes downward guiltily. *What do I say now,* he wondered. He decided to sidestep her last comment completely. "How about your brother?"

"Byung-Wah? Oh, he's out, as always," Gin-Yung said. "He just turned sixteen. He hates living with all us girls."

Again the room fell silent. Todd looked around and spotted a framed picture of himself with his arm around Gin-Yung on an end table. He tried to remember where it had been taken or what the occasion might have been. But he couldn't place it. *It seems so long ago,* Todd thought. *How could I have cleared Gin-Yung out of my mind like that?* When an image of Elizabeth Wakefield flashed before him, a shiver went up his spine. *Keep your focus, Wilkins. Don't slip up—not now.*

"So . . . what classes are you going to sign up for? You *are* coming back next semester, aren't you?"

"I—I haven't had a chance yet," Gin-Yung said, shifting slightly in her seat. Her foot tapped nervously. "You know, London was a really interesting place."

"Oh yeah, London. Tell me about it," Todd suggested, glad that she seemed to want to change the course of the conversation, even if it sounded forced. "How was the internship?"

"Exhausting. But the best part of my job was the trips. I got to travel all over the country to watch football—you know, soccer matches. I think I did more sightseeing than actual reporting. I even got to go to Spain one weekend."

"Spain? Wow, no kidding."

"It was incredible, Todd. The most beautiful place I'd ever seen. Remember how we talked about going there once? I said I always wanted to see a bullfight and you . . ." Suddenly Gin-Yung's animated chatter faded away, and she visibly shivered.

"Are you cold?" Todd asked. He moved from the couch and knelt beside the recliner. *Or are you upset because you're remembering a time when we were happy together?* he added silently.

"No, I'm fine."

"Oh. OK. So what were you saying about Spain?"

"I—I forgot. It wasn't important anyway. I was just rambling. . . ." She trailed off, slapping her palms rhythmically against the sides of the recliner as if she were marking time. Suddenly she stopped. "Hey, I know. I've got something for you. Wait till you see what it is."

Gin-Yung bolted up from the recliner and stumbled a little as she walked to a nearby closet. She opened the door and tried to pull out a big cardboard box, but she slipped and fell.

"Are you OK?" Todd exclaimed, leaping from the couch and running over to help her up.

"See where these girly clothes get me?" She laughed as she dusted herself off. "Why anyone would *want* to wear stuff like this is beyond me." Undaunted, she reached for the box and tried to pull it out again, her arms visibly shaking from the strain.

"Here, Gin. Let me get that for you." With a grunt Todd lifted the heavy box and carried it over to the coffee table. "What is it? You didn't lug this thing all the way back from England, did you?"

"Open it," she said.

"You really didn't have to get me anything," he remarked as he ripped layers of masking tape off the lid.

"It's not really a gift," Gin-Yung told him while he tore off the last of the tape. "Now that you're back on the basketball team, I knew you'd want to have these."

Todd couldn't believe his eyes when he opened the box. "Oh, man! My trophies! My high-school letters and posters too! I thought all this stuff was long gone." His heart pounded excitedly when he picked up one of his old high-school basketball trophies. The ornament at the top was a little bent, but it was *his*. "This is unbelievable, Gin. Where did you find these?"

"I didn't. Don't you remember the day you tried to get rid of them? You were so ticked about being thrown off the team that you threw all your sports mementos into this box. I was with you that day."

Todd remembered it well. He thought his

world had come to an end that day. After a point-fixing scandal rocked the SVU basketball team, he'd been unfairly denied readmission to the athletics program—even though he hadn't been a part of the scandal. He'd packed up every painful reminder and begged Gin-Yung to get rid of the box.

"I didn't leave it in the Dumpster like you asked." Gin-Yung smiled shyly. "I brought it home with me instead. I knew you'd want it all back one day."

Todd shook his head in amazement. *How can I break up with her after something like this?* he wondered. *Maybe I can't.* For a moment he couldn't speak. Finally he swallowed the lump in his throat and quietly said, "I guess you know me pretty well."

Gin-Yung shrugged as if she didn't know how to respond. "I'm . . . I'm so glad to see you again, Todd. You look even better than I remembered."

"It's good to see you too." Todd stopped himself before returning her compliment—it would have been a lie. Now that he was standing close to her, he could see that she didn't look good at all. In fact, she looked worn out and thin. *I hope she hasn't been worrying about me too much,* he thought. *If I decide to go back to Elizabeth, I'll just end up disappointing her even more.*

"Todd . . ." Gin-Yung headed back for the

recliner and laughed nervously. "I guess I should get to the point, shouldn't I?"

"About what?" Todd sank back down on the couch, dreading what Gin-Yung was going to say next.

"About me . . . and you. It seems like—and I think you feel the same way—like we really need to sort things out."

"You're right," Todd said, feeling somewhat relieved. "I'm glad you think so too."

"I mean, a lot's happened since I left for London. And we really need to talk about that."

That sounds pretty ominous, Todd thought, his ears ringing. Did Gin somehow suspect—or maybe even *know*—that he had gotten back together with Elizabeth? That would explain Kim's strange behavior earlier. *But if Gin-Yung did know, she'd probably be upset—more so than she seems right now,* Todd reassured himself.

"So . . . do you want to talk?" Gin-Yung looked expectant, but strangely calm.

"Sure," Todd replied. "You know, I was wondering where we were sitting now—the two of us, I mean."

To his amazement, Gin-Yung raised her eyebrows and giggled. "In my living room, silly."

Todd's forehead creased for a moment before he realized that Gin-Yung was joking. He laughed easily, welcoming the sudden change in mood.

Todd glanced over at her and saw that even though her skin was pale and drawn, her eyes were bright. *This* was the Gin-Yung he remembered—the quick-thinking, high-spirited woman who'd helped him through so many dark times. *If she can still joke like that, then she* can't *know about me and Elizabeth,* he realized confidently.

Gin-Yung waved her hands in front of her face as if to erase her last words. "I'm sorry. That was a stupid thing to say. I guess I'm a little nervous."

"Well, you seem a lot less nervous than I feel," Todd admitted.

Gin-Yung shot him a sympathetic look, but she seemed to deflate a little. It was almost as if she were shrinking into the big recliner. "I've known for a while that this little talk would be coming. But that doesn't make it any easier, does it?"

"No, it doesn't." *What am I going to do,* he thought anxiously. *Any moment now she's going to ask me how I feel. And I just don't know. Gin-Yung means so much to me, but . . . maybe I should come right out and tell her about Liz.* After all Gin-Yung had done for him, she at least deserved his honesty. But did she deserve to have her heart broken?

"I'll go first," Gin-Yung offered, much to Todd's relief. "I'll just come right out and say it. I've been hiding something from you."

Todd's eyes widened. "What is it?"

"While I was in London, something happened. Lots of things happened." She took a deep breath and let it out. "Oh, Todd, this is really hard for me."

"It's OK, Gin. You can tell me anything."

"I—I met someone, Todd. A guy. And it's . . . it's pretty serious."

Todd blinked. Were his ears deceiving him? Nothing Gin-Yung could have said would have surprised him more.

"Now, I know that when I left for London, we agreed that it was OK for us to date other people. We knew that keeping a long-distance relationship would be tough."

Todd squirmed. "I remember."

"I'm sorry I didn't tell you sooner," she continued, her words seeming to flow a lot more easily than they had before. "But I just felt like I had to do it in person. We can't see each other anymore, Todd. I . . . I wouldn't feel right about it."

"Who is it?" Todd asked lamely, knowing full well he wouldn't know the guy.

"His name is James. He's a soccer player. I really love him, Todd." Gin-Yung's hands trembled, as if it truly hurt her to be revealing this news to him. "Please don't be angry with me."

"I'm not angry, just surprised. I mean, you said you weren't going back to London. Is he coming here?"

She shook her head. "I don't know what's going to happen with me and James, but either way I can't very well keep seeing you when I'm in love with someone else. It wouldn't be fair."

Gin-Yung's words resounded sharply in Todd's ears. Guilt crawled through him slowly and clutched at this stomach. "No, I guess not."

"Todd," Gin-Yung said, her eyes openly pleading. "I need to ask you something. And I want you to be totally honest with me."

"OK." Todd swallowed hard. *Here it comes,* he thought.

"You never stopped loving Elizabeth Wakefield, did you?"

His heart stopped cold. "Why—"

"I know about you and Elizabeth, Todd. You don't have to lie to me."

When Todd looked into Gin-Yung's eyes, he knew that his expression would be giving him away. But instead of appearing bitter or heart-broken, Todd was stunned to see that Gin-Yung looked satisfied. A little glad, even.

"I was going to tell you, Gin, but—"

Gin-Yung raised a hand to stop him. "There's no need to explain. I know just how you feel."

"How?"

She leaned forward in her chair and looked at him almost clinically. "Let's face it, Todd. We had some great times together, but I think we confused friendship with being in love."

My thoughts exactly, Todd realized. The clenching feeling in his chest began to ease.

"I mean, when two people are comfortable together and they spend enough time with each other, you know, they naturally assume what they're feeling is love."

"But I did love you, Gin-Yung." Todd had to let her know. She seemed a little too matter-of-fact about the whole thing, as if she were dissecting the idea rather than discussing it. There was no emotion, no sense of loss or regret.

"Maybe. But not the same way you loved Elizabeth Wakefield."

You do *know me all too well, Gin,* he said silently.

She continued. "At one point I honestly believed I loved you too. And maybe I did. But now I've come to realize that we were just kidding ourselves."

This is unbelievable, Todd thought. *Has Gin-Yung been reading my mind?*

"It's better this way, Todd. As much as I enjoyed being with you, I always felt as if Elizabeth was there, haunting us. I know you've never been able to fully let go of her."

Todd nodded. He couldn't deny it—not when Gin-Yung was being so straight with him.

"If you want to go back to Elizabeth, go

ahead. I want you to. But you have to do one last thing for me."

"What's that?" Todd asked nervously. Even though his heart was soaring, he knew that there had to be a catch in there somewhere.

Gin-Yung stood up and walked over to where he sat, slowly and deliberately. She held out her arms. "Give me one last hug, Todd, for old times' sake."

Gladly Todd jumped from his seat and swept Gin-Yung up in his arms. She seemed lighter and thinner than he remembered, but he figured that was because he was feeling so relieved. Her heart pounded quickly against his chest.

"I'm so happy we both feel the same way, Gin," Todd said gratefully as he let her go. "I'd been so afraid to tell you about me and Liz. I didn't want to hurt you. I just hope this guy—"

"James."

"Right, James. I hope he makes you happy, Gin. You deserve it. I'm sorry I couldn't be the one."

"We just weren't right for each other, I guess," she said with a wistful smile. "I guess it's better that we found out now."

"Exactly."

They stood quietly for a moment, and Todd began to get the feeling that Gin-Yung wanted him to leave. She kept shooting glances over at the cardboard box on the coffee table.

"I guess I'd better go."

"OK."

Todd picked up the heavy box and made his way toward the door. "Thanks, Gin. For everything."

"You're welcome," she said softly, turning away just before Todd bounded for the door and ran out to his car.

Gin-Yung really is something else, he thought as he tossed the box in the passenger seat and rushed to start the car. The first thing he wanted to do was to find a phone and call Elizabeth.

He patted the cardboard box and grinned. "Thanks again, Gin-Yung," he said out loud. "Thanks for giving me back my past." And he meant much more than the basketball trophies.

As soon as she heard Todd's car roar out of the driveway Gin-Yung collapsed onto the couch. She felt completely wrung out from hiding her emotions for so long. *What have you done?* she asked herself as she gave in to the tears that had been threatening to fall through her whole ordeal. *Todd's the only man you ever loved, and you lied to him. You lied to him and sent him away—to love someone else. Why? Why didn't you—*

"Why didn't you tell Todd the *truth?*"

At first Gin-Yung thought the voice was her own. But the sheer force of it made her jump.

164

When she looked up, she realized that her sister was standing in front of her, hands on her hips.

"What were you *thinking*, Gin? What made you come up with those stupid stories?"

Gin-Yung was shattered. She couldn't believe her sister had violated her privacy at a time like this. "How could you spy on me, Kim?"

"I had to!" Kim threw herself down on the couch next to her. "I didn't know what would happen—what might happen to you. I thought you were going to tell him the truth, Gin. I wasn't expecting to hear about *James*. And I'm even more surprised that Todd actually *bought* it!"

Gin-Yung sniffed. "I told him what he wanted to hear, that's all." She shook her head sadly, her sense of loss growing with every passing second. "He must really love her, Kim. If he was willing to accept my lies so easily . . . he must really love her."

"I'm just as upset about that as you are. But you can't think about that now. You have to think about what you've just done. You lied to him, and now he's gone."

And now he's gone. The words reverberated in Gin-Yung's head. She had to keep talking—if she didn't, the echo would make her go crazy. "I had to lie to him. I had no other choice."

"But if you told him the truth, he'd probably still be here now instead of driving off to see—"

"I know that," Gin-Yung interrupted, not wanting to hear the rest of Kim's sentence. "I know that if I told him everything, he'd still be my boyfriend. That's the problem."

"Problem?" Kim rolled her eyes. "I don't get you at all, Gin."

"How many times do I have to tell you? I care about Todd too much to—to force him to be with me when he doesn't really *want* to be."

"If you really care about him, then you should tell him everything. It's not too late."

"No! I can't!" Gin-Yung's voice broke in anguish. She was afraid to continue—afraid of where this conversation was leading. "Todd doesn't love me anymore, Kim. He loves Elizabeth Wakefield. I don't want him around pretending that he loves me out of obligation or . . . whatever."

"Is that what you really want, Gin? Is it right that Todd can run off, guilt-free, and enjoy himself while you sit here and suffer?"

"Stop!" Gin-Yung cried, putting her hands over her ears. "Please, I don't want to think about it!"

"How could you lie to him so easily, Gin?"

A blazing pain shot through Gin-Yung's spine, and hot tears returned to her eyes. "It *wasn't* easy! It was the hardest thing I've ever done in my life! You have no idea how painful it was, Kim! No idea!"

166

"It sure was painful for me to listen to."

Gin-Yung couldn't believe what she'd just heard. "How could you say something like that? What would *you* have done if you were in my place? You'd *have* to lie to him. Because you wouldn't be able to tell him the truth. You'd be too scared to say it out loud!"

When the impact of her own words sank in and she saw her sister's face turn white, the realization of what was happening to Gin-Yung hit her like a hammer. Her entire body lurched with blinding pain. She curled up in a ball, heaving and shaking with fear. "I'm too scared to say it out loud," she repeated, barely above a whisper. "Oh, Kim, please listen to me. Please hold me."

Kim's arms closed around her. "Gin," Kim said soothingly, "I'm not trying to be mean. I just . . . I just hate watching you fall apart like this."

Gin-Yung straightened up and fell against her sister. Kim held her tight, as if to control the violent, racking sobs that Gin-Yung was casting into her shoulder. *This can't be happening to me,* Gin-Yung thought, choking on her own tears. *I don't want to believe it. How can I tell Todd the truth when I can't even accept it myself?*

Chapter Nine

"Feeling hungry, darling?" Bobby Hornet asked, his eyebrows arched in amusement. "Hang in there. We'll have our food in"—he held up two fingers—"two shakes."

Jessica sank back into the plush leather limousine seat and felt her face turn red. Not with embarrassment but with annoyance. Just as Bobby Hornet's long white limo pulled up in front of Marvioso, the trendy Italian bistro, Jessica's stomach growled loudly. But Bobby, casually dangling a champagne glass in his hand, had mistaken it as a signal for hunger. And Jessica Wakefield *hated* being misunderstood.

I'm nervous, *not hungry,* she said silently. *And I'm not ready for this night at* all.

"Hey, pa-pa-*ra*-zzi," Bobby drawled as he looked out the limo's smoked glass windows.

Masterfully he ran his hands through his long hair, working the dark waves of his trademark mane so that just a few long strands hung in front of his left eye. "Prepare yourself, Jessica. Looks like we're going to get snapped."

Great. Jessica prayed that the color of her face wouldn't match the shimmering scarlet slip dress she'd borrowed from Lila in the paparazzi's pictures.

Pictures. "Pictures!" Jessica gasped aloud. But there *couldn't* be any pictures—they'd be evidence of her dinner with Bobby Hornet! Jessica shuddered at the thought of Nick discovering her night's infidelity on the gossip page of a glossy mag.

"Something wrong, Miss Scarlet?" Bobby inquired with an easy, blindingly white smile.

"No pictures," was all she could squeak out.

"No pictures?" Bobby asked. "What are you—on the run from the law or something?"

That's one way of putting it, Jessica thought, her stomach now sinking instead of growling.

Bobby laughed heartily. "That's pretty funny, Jessica. Here you are afraid to get your picture taken, and that's what this whole night is all about. Or have you already forgotten the charity calendar?"

Oops. "Well, um, I'm just not prepared. I mean, *look* at me!"

Bobby perused her from head to toe: the

loosely flowing blond hair; the scarlet slip dress and matching, whisper-thin silk wrap; the same pumps she'd worn the previous afternoon in the music store—for good luck, of course. Jessica could tell from the look on Bobby's face that he *wasn't* buying it.

"Sorry, but I don't see anything wrong." He winked, and Jessica couldn't help but feel a tiny twinge of pride. But her brief feelings of confidence vanished when Bobby said, "Well, here we go!"

Suddenly the back door of the limo opened, and Bobby jumped out. The driver's gloved hand reached inside to drag Jessica into certain doom.

Think fast, girl. Instinctively Jessica took off the silk wrap and wound it around her head, obscuring her hair and most of the bottom half of her face. She snatched a pair of sunglasses from her purse, threw them on, and jumped out to accept her fate.

As she emerged from the limo people were already shouting Bobby's name. He seemed to be taking it all in stride—after all, this kind of thing must happen to him every day. But suddenly all the attention turned to her. Flashbulbs popped and reporters began hollering, "Mystery woman! Over here!"

Jessica didn't dare look in any direction other than the door of the restaurant. With her hand held in front of her face she dashed toward the entrance and let herself in, not even waiting for Bobby to get there first. By the time Bobby made his way inside, Jessica had replaced her wrap, fixed her hair, and stashed her shades back in her purse.

Bobby casually placed a hand on Jessica's waist, and she jumped. If this had been one of her pre–Nick Fox days, Jessica would have eaten the whole situation up. Here she was with a famous musician—a guy who happened to be the third most intriguing man in America, according to *Celebrity Searchlight* magazine. Total strangers fawned before him, falling over themselves to take a picture or get an autograph. And Jessica Wakefield was right there in the spotlight with him.

But tonight she didn't want to be in the spotlight. She wanted to slink off into a dark corner and get the whole thing over with.

Jessica ducked her head slightly so that her hair covered her face as the two of them followed the maitre d' through the maze of hanging plants and stained-glass lampshades. When she realized they were being led toward the enormous picture windows up front, she paused and turned to Bobby.

"Don't you think we should sit in the back, where it's more private?"

"Are you kidding? With you looking like a Christmas package wrapped in hundred-dollar bills? We're sitting right up front where everyone can see you for themselves."

And he meant it. The table he had requested was right in the center of a bay window. If not for the glass, they'd practically be sitting in the middle of the sidewalk!

After dismissing the maitre d' with a generous tip, Bobby took Jessica's silk wrap and seated her in a chair facing the street. She felt like she'd been dropped into an aquarium at the zoo.

"Wouldn't you rather sit over here and enjoy the view?" she asked as he settled into the chair across from her.

"I have all the view I need from right here."

His stare sent a shiver up Jessica's spine. "But Bobby," Jessica pleaded, "I'm sure all your fans out there would rather look at *you*."

"No way. I'd prefer to put you on display. Think of it as a city beautification project."

Jessica was flattered by Bobby's comments, but she couldn't truly enjoy them. She was too busy staring through the window at the street outside. If Nick—or any of his uniformed coworkers—happened to cruise down the boulevard, she'd be sunk.

And for what? A chance to get her picture in a charity calendar? Jessica couldn't believe she'd let herself go this far over something that seemed so pathetically small when compared to her feelings for Nick. And even worse, from the look in Bobby's eyes she was beginning to suspect that he was hungry for more than just dinner.

Jessica snapped to attention when Bobby went ahead and ordered a cocktail for himself, a spring water for her, and an assortment of appetizers and entrées for both of them. She was a little piqued that Bobby didn't ask her what she would have liked, but in the end she didn't care. She knew her insides were too knotted up to digest anything anyway.

When a waitress appeared instantly with their drinks, Bobby turned to Jessica and made a sad puppy-dog face. "Jessica, what's wrong? Where's that adorable dimple I fell for yesterday?"

Jessica forced herself to smile.

"Ah, there it is. You're so beautiful."

"I must seem kind of plain after all the models and movie stars you usually date."

He made a disdainful face. "That's all publicity. When I saw you walk down those stairs in that bikini, my contact lenses nearly melted."

Jessica winced at the image. "All I wanted was to get your attention," she said quietly.

"Oh, you got it, all right. I haven't stopped thinking about it."

A waitress arrived with a tray of antipasto. Bobby dug in as if he hadn't eaten for days, but Jessica sat back meekly and sipped her water.

"Eat up, Jessica! Weren't you hungry before? Here, try this prosciutto. It's Marvioso's specialty."

Jessica took a piece of the thinly sliced Italian ham, dropped it onto her plate, and left it there.

"Oh no," Bobby groaned. "You aren't one of those model types who are always on a diet, are you? I hate that."

"No, I—"

"Well, then, you must be a vegetarian. Here you go." Bobby scooped up a marinated mushroom, an artichoke heart, and a black olive and laid them gently on her plate.

The olive looked the least threatening, so she popped it into her mouth, chewed, and swallowed. It might as well have been a pencil eraser for all the enjoyment she got out of it. And on top of it all, it seemed to grow on its way down. Soon her stomach felt as if she had swallowed a tennis ball.

"That's my girl." Bobby reached over and gave Jessica's arm a gentle stroke with his fingertip.

This feels so wrong, Jessica thought feverishly. *If Nick knew what I was doing right now, it would kill him. How could I deceive him like this? I practically owe him my life.*

If it weren't for Nick, she would probably be in jail right now. After they'd first started dating, he'd mistakenly arrested her in a drug bust. Nick had been furious at her for violating his trust—even though she'd been completely innocent! But when Nick finally got the evidence proving that Jessica wasn't guilty, his trust in her had been restored. After that horrible incident she'd hoped he would never have a reason to lose faith in her again.

And just look at me now, Jessica thought, disgusted with herself. *Guilty as sin. Maybe I should* confess this to Nick before it's too late. *Maybe he'd even forgive me. He* is *the best boyfriend in the world, after all.* She smiled, thinking of Nick's gorgeous green eyes and the wild, reckless way he rode his Triumph motorcycle. *That's what I'll do. I'll get through this dinner and tell Nick everything the first chance I get. After all, it's only dinner.*

Bobby sipped his cocktail and smiled. "How should we pose in the calendar, Jessica? What sort of scene would suit you? I know—we can pose in a gondola. I'll serenade you in the moonlight. . . ."

At the realization that Bobby was essentially *giving* her the calendar spot right then and there, Jessica's mind went into overdrive. *Uh-oh. Now Bobby will expect more from you for sure,* she told herself, her pulse pounding madly in her ears. *First there's the innocent little dinner. Then he'll take you out dancing at a club. After that a late-night ride in the limo. And then . . . and then . . .* And then Nick would get his heart broken—and so would she.

I can't go through with this, she thought urgently. *I have to draw the line, and I can't wait another minute. This has to stop* now.

"I'm sorry, Bobby, I just can't do this," Jessica blurted.

"Then try the black olives."

"No, I don't mean the antipasto. I mean, I can't go through with *this.*"

"With what, doll?"

"This!" She waved her arms around her wildly, not wanting to have to say the word *date.*

"If you don't like Italian food, you should have said something. We could always go somewhere else."

Jessica let out an exasperated groan. "It's not the food. It's . . ." She trailed off, knowing that what she was about to say would most certainly and irrevocably ruin her chances of being in the calendar. But if it meant keeping Nick, it'd all be worth it. She took a deep breath and went for the plunge. "Bobby, I have to tell you something. I—I have a boyfriend."

He laughed. "Well, I'm not surprised. I'd be shocked if you didn't have a stableful."

"No, I mean, I have a *serious* boyfriend. And he—he means everything to me."

"I see," Bobby said, swirling his cocktail around in little circles.

"Look, this was a bad idea." Jessica reached

for the silk wrap and put it on in preparation to leave. "I just made a mistake, that's all. A *big* mistake. And I'm sorry I wasted your time, Bobby. If—"

Jessica stopped herself, not knowing if she should actually say what she was about to say. The very *idea* of speaking the words out loud made her deathly ill. And if she actually managed to choke them out—well, she had no choice but to face the consequences. Jessica had to do it—for Nick's sake.

Gripping a fork until her knuckles turned white, Jessica swallowed her pride and spoke. "I wouldn't blame you, Bobby, if you decided to give the spot to Alison Quinn now. In fact, I'd totally understand." There, she'd said it. And she was amazed to see that she was still in one piece when she was finished.

"Hey! Hey, calm down," Bobby replied, reaching across the table and putting his hand on hers soothingly. "There's no need to get upset. Besides, it wrinkles your pretty face. Surely that boyfriend of yours wouldn't begrudge you a little pasta, now, would he? After all, you gotta eat."

"I'm sorry, but—oh no. Oh no, no, no!"

"What is it, love?" He gripped her hand tightly, as if to chain her to the table.

Jessica could hardly believe her awful luck. Coming slowly down the boulevard was a police cruiser, its familiar black-and-white markings moving closer with each passing second. Jessica sat frozen in place, paralyzed, unable to extract her hand from Bobby's iron grip as the entire cruiser came into view. From a distance she couldn't tell what the driver looked like. But as it drew closer the blissfully unaware face of Nick Fox came into focus in the driver's-side window.

"Aaargh! Let go of me! Let go of me!" Jessica shrieked, trying desperately to jerk her hand away from his.

"Are you having some kind of attack, dear?"

But before Bobby let go of her hand, the police car screeched to a halt directly in front of the bay window. Jessica suddenly found herself staring into Nick's eyes. She felt caged in, trapped—she was in for it now.

As if in slow motion Nick's handsome features twisted into a grimace of surprise and hurt. Soon the surprise faded, only to be replaced by sheer, unadulterated anger.

Jessica jumped to her feet, not caring that she knocked over a water carafe in the process. It smashed to the floor, but she hardly noticed.

"Jess, what is it?"

"There's my boyfriend. I have to go!"

Bobby reached out for her, but she dodged his grasp. As she turned to make a break for it she was stopped in her tracks. *He's holding me against my will, Nick!* she cried silently. She spun around, perfectly willing to fight Bobby off if she had to, but instead she discovered that Lila's silk wrap had gotten tangled around the chair. Frantically she jerked it loose and dragged it along behind her as she ran for the door as quickly as she could in her high heels.

Finally she burst through the doors, screaming, "Nick!" But it was too late. "Please, Nick! Wait!" she screamed as the cruiser sped away, leaving her standing on the sidewalk alone, with Lila's silk wrap fluttering around her like a red flag of defeat.

Hearing a key in the door, Tom looked up from the stack of books and papers he'd spread across the Conroys' dining table. *It's about time!* he thought. He was beginning to worry about Mr. Conroy. It wasn't like him to go out for so long and leave Jake and Mary alone. Of course, they hadn't been alone the past two hours since Tom had arrived, but Mr. Conroy hadn't known that. Tom was just glad he had decided to show up at the condo early and keep his half siblings company.

"Tom, you're early!" Mr. Conroy said cheerfully. He was balancing two large white sacks of takeout food as he stuffed the keys back into his pocket. "It's Hannah's night off," he said, referring to the family's cook/housekeeper/baby-sitter.

"So I had to go out and rustle up some grub." He proudly held up the sacks.

Two hours is an awfully long time to get take-out, Tom thought, but he trusted his father's judgment. "Let me move my books, and I'll set the table," he offered.

"No, don't bother. We can all eat at the small table in the kitchen. Where are the kids?"

"Jake is playing video games."

"Of course. Why did I bother to ask?"

"And Mary is practicing her cello."

"No surprise there either. As much as that girl practices, you'd think she was getting paid by the hour."

Mr. Conroy yelled for Jake and Mary to wash their hands and come to the kitchen. "I have a special surprise dinner." He set the packages of food on the table while Tom got the plates.

"What is it?" asked Jake, Tom's eight-year-old half brother, as he tore open the nearest bag. He turned up his pug nose. "Oh, darn, I wanted pizza."

"And I wanted tacos," ten-year-old Mary complained, pulling out her chair.

"We always have pizza or tacos when Hannah is out," Mr. Conroy reminded them.

"Right," they cried in unison, "'cause that's what we *want*."

"Well, it's time we had something different.

You kids need to eat something more nutritious. I've been letting you two get away with murder lately as far as food is concerned."

Tom set plates around the table while Mr. Conroy carefully arranged the soggy-looking cardboard cartons in the center.

"I got these at the Organic Palace," George said.

Tom winced and nearly dropped one of the gold-rimmed glasses he was taking from the cabinet—not because he was disgusted by the prospect of a macrobiotic dinner, but because he was all too familiar with the Organic Palace chain of health-food stores. There was one right near the SVU campus, and he remembered that it was Eliz—his ex-girlfriend's favorite place to buy fresh vegetables and fruits.

Jake leaned over the table and stared into the largest carton. "What's this gunk?"

"*That* is vegetarian rice and nut casserole," Mr. Conroy said, reaching over Jake's grimacing face to stick a serving spoon into the beige goo. "And this is blanched broccoli. And here we have sautéed tofu and carrot health salad."

If George is waiting for someone to shout, "Yummy!" he's going to be disappointed, Tom thought bemusedly. Jake and Mary looked sick, and Tom wasn't feeling so good himself.

Mr. Conroy opened the last bag and dumped

a warm, brown loaf onto a plate. "Seven-grain dark bread. Fresh from the oven," he said with a flourish. "Try it, you'll like it."

Mary crossed her arms over her chest. "No, I won't. I'll puke."

"Tom's not eating his," Jake whined. "So I'm not neither."

"Not *either*, Jake," Mr. Conroy corrected him. "Now, Tom, would you please do me a favor and set a good example for your little brother and sister?"

Tom grinned. He loved to hear that phrase: brother and sister. It reminded him that he had a real family again—a family who loved him and was becoming more important to him with each passing day. He couldn't imagine life without them.

To prove his feelings, he would have eaten cardboard—*which is exactly what this bread tastes like*, he thought as he shoved the end piece into his mouth and began to chew . . . and chew.

"There—see, kids?" Mr. Conroy pointed out. "Your big brother likes it. This kind of bread is better for you. It's full of fiber."

Yeah, enough fiber to thatch a roof, Tom thought.

"I have to go practice some more." Mary pushed her chair away from the table.

"Sit," George commanded gently. "Eat."

Mary scooted back in her chair and stared at

her plate. "Dana's going to be maaad," she warned in a lightly teasing voice as she began to push the broccoli around with her fork.

"Speaking of Dana," Tom began, hoping to defuse any further confrontations, "I went to her recital Thursday night. She had a cello solo that stole the show."

"Why didn't you take me?" Mary cried, looking almost hurt. "I wanted to see her play."

"Not me," Jake added. "*Blecch*. I think I'd rather eat this junk instead."

"Mary, Tom probably had a date," Mr. Conroy explained.

"I did, actually," Tom replied proudly. "With Dana."

"Really?" Mary exclaimed. "That's so cool! Have you kissed her yet?"

Jake laughed and wrapped his arms around himself. "Tom lo-oves Da-na! Tom lo-oves Da-na!" he sang while he made kissy faces.

"Stop it, you two." Mr. Conroy smiled and cleared his throat. "Dana's a nice girl, Tom. And I'm glad that you're finally going out again and enjoying yourself. But I didn't think she was your type, exactly."

"Well, she is," Tom replied, surprised at his father's reaction. "She's a lot of fun, George. She's so free and uninhibited and creative. . . ." He trailed off as he recalled their incredible date yesterday and the pleased look that came into her wide-set eyes when he kissed her. "I love being with Dana. She makes me happy. She's helping me to—to forget."

"I'm glad Tom likes Dana," Mary said as she nibbled on a piece of bread. "I hope they get married. Then I can play duets with her whenever I want."

"Now, let's not rush into things." Mr. Conroy chuckled amiably, but his face soon turned serious. "I'm glad too, Tom. But—"

"But what?"

Mr. Conroy put down his fork. "What about Elizabeth?"

Tom's stomach turned. "What *about* Elizabeth?" he asked in astonishment. "What does this have to do with her? She and I are finished, George. I thought I made that clear."

"Yes, you did. But . . . well, think of how she must feel. Does she know you're dating someone else already?"

"What do I care?" Tom was amazed to hear his father pressing the issue so strongly. "*You* were the one who was so big on me going out and having a good time. Elizabeth's feelings don't matter to me anymore. After what she did to us—"

"I know, Tom, but you can't keep blaming her for what happened. She was just feeling a little jealous of the attention you were giving me and the kids, that's all."

"How can you defend her like that?"

"I don't know, Tom. I guess . . . I guess I feel a little guilty over what happened between you two."

"*Guilty?* After what she said about you?" Tom looked over at Jake and Mary before continuing any further. They were busy daring each other to try the food and completely ignoring the discussion at hand. Tom lowered his voice to a whisper. "She accused you of coming on to her, George. That's completely unforgivable."

"I'm not talking about that. It's just that if I never came into your life, you two would still be together. You seemed so right for each other. I hate thinking that you broke up just because of me."

"George, how can you think that? I broke up with Elizabeth because she's a no-good liar. It was bound to happen someday. I'm better off without her. In fact, I wish I'd never met her."

"If not for Elizabeth, Tom, you and I might never have found each other. You have to at least give her a little credit."

Tom had to admit to himself that his father was right in that respect. But he wasn't about to give in. "I can't do that. Not after what she did to us."

"I've found it in my heart to forgive her, even though she may never find that out," Mr. Conroy said. "I just wish that you could do the same."

185

"I'll never forgive her," Tom stated with force. "Besides, that's not even an issue anymore. I've found someone new. Dana's been really good for me. And I think . . . I think I may be falling in love with her. Can't you be happy for me?"

Mr. Conroy opened his mouth as if to say something, but instead he silently reached for the blanched broccoli and dished a generous helping of it onto his plate.

"Please, George. I'm trying to start my life over now. I need your support more than anything. Why can't you be on my side?"

Mr. Conroy suddenly seemed far away, as if he were lost in thought. After a few more moments of silence he shook his head and began to laugh softly. "Oh, I'm just an old fool," he said. "I don't want to fight with you, son. Of course I'm on your side. If you're in love with Dana, then I couldn't be happier for you."

Tom took a deep, cleansing breath. "Thanks, George. I really needed to hear that."

Mr. Conroy reached over and patted Tom on the back. "I'll never bring Elizabeth up again, I promise. It's really none of my business. You should be free to date whomever you choose."

Sighing with relief, Tom remembered the big day he'd planned with Dana. "Speaking of dates, I need to ask you a favor. Can I borrow your convertible tomorrow? Dana and I are going to take a drive along the coast, and it'd be great with the top down."

"Of course. I'd be more than happy to loan it to you." Mr. Conroy got to his feet. "Let me get the keys."

"You don't have to get up. Just tell me where they are. I'll get them."

"Sit tight, Tom. It'd be a lot simpler if I got them myself."

As Mr. Conroy cheerfully walked out of the kitchen Tom felt terrible about arguing with him. After all, the fact that his father was so ready to forgive Elizabeth after her vicious accusations was proof that he was a genuinely giving and selfless man. His willingness to lend out his gold Mercedes convertible was just more evidence of his generous nature.

I should really go after him and apologize, Tom realized. *Without Jake and Mary around, it'll be a lot easier for me to let him know how I feel.*

"'Scuse me, kids," Tom said, putting his napkin on the table. "I'll be right back." He headed out of the kitchen and noticed that the door to Mr. Conroy's study was open. He could see shadows moving along the wall.

Tom peered inside and saw his father taking a set of keys from his antique oak rolltop desk. But when Tom tapped on the door frame gently, Mr. Conroy jumped up and slammed down the rolltop so quickly a nearby lamp rattled.

"Sorry," Tom apologized. "I didn't mean to scare you."

"Oh, that's OK," he replied. "I've just been working a little too hard lately at the patent office. I must be really exhausted to be jumping at the sound of my own children." Mr. Conroy looked perfectly composed when he met Tom in the doorway, but Tom sensed that his father's nerves were probably a little too rattled to handle another heavy discussion.

"Here are the keys. Drive the convertible home tonight if you'd like." Mr. Conroy held the key ring out magnanimously, and Tom took it. "Just bring it back after your date tomorrow night, OK? I'll need it Monday morning."

"No problem. It may be late, though."

"Don't worry about it. If no one's around when you get to the house, just leave the keys on the kitchen table where I can find them. I promised the kids we'd go see that new Disney movie tomorrow night."

Tom chuckled. "You must be thrilled."

"All those cute singing animals? Are you kidding?"

"I'm sure you'll have a great time." He jingled the keys in his hand. "Thanks, Dad."

Tom's chest filled with warmth when he suddenly realized what he'd said: *Dad.* He'd never called Mr. Conroy that before. After his adoptive father was killed, Tom figured he'd never be able to call anyone Dad again—not even Mr. Conroy. The word held so much importance for him. But it just slipped out so easily, without his even having to think about it.

"Anytime, son," Mr. Conroy said proudly. He didn't say anything about what Tom had just called him, but the gleam in his eyes told Tom everything.

"Look, I'm really sorry about what happened earlier," Tom said hastily. "It still bothers me a little to hear Elizabeth's name. I can't help it."

"Don't give it a second thought. It won't happen again." George Conroy clasped his arm around Tom's shoulders as they turned and walked back to the kitchen. "Now, let's go finish our dinner, shall we?"

Both Tom and his father burst out laughing when they returned to the kitchen table. Mary and Jake were sitting there with overly innocent looks on their faces, their plates magically cleaned. All the health-food cartons on the table were overflowing, as if more food had been messily scooped back into them.

"Can we have our dessert now?" Jake asked, his eyes wide but gleaming impishly.

Mr. Conroy took a long look at his untouched plate of tofu, broccoli, and gluey beige casserole. "I don't think so, kids." He walked to the phone and made a call. "Hello, Jay's Pizza? I'd like to order two large pies. With everything."

Chapter Ten

On Sunday morning, Dickenson Hall was as still and quiet as Sleeping Beauty's castle after the spell had been cast. Even Gin-Yung's loafers were noiseless as they slid along the dingy carpeting.

Gin-Yung stopped before door number 28 and took a deep breath. *If last night was the hardest thing I ever had to do . . . well, this is going to be the second hardest,* she thought as she tapped lightly on the door. *There's no turning back now.*

The door opened, and a sleepy Elizabeth Wakefield stood in front of her.

Gin-Yung sighed. *How can anyone look that great when they first wake up? No wonder Todd loves Elizabeth. She's perfect.*

Surprise flickered across Elizabeth's face.

"Gin-Yung . . . hi," she said as a sad crease formed between her eyebrows.

Why should she look sad? Gin-Yung wondered. *She should be overjoyed to have Todd all to herself again. No, she's probably just disappointed to see me instead of him.* "Hi, Elizabeth," she said as calmly as she could. "I'm sorry if I woke you."

"That's OK," Elizabeth said quietly.

Gin-Yung peeked inside the semidark room. If a giant white stripe had been painted down the center, the territory of each twin couldn't have been more clearly marked. One side of the narrow dorm room looked as if an entire closetful of clothes had been dumped on it. But the other side was perfectly neat—even the bed. Gin-Yung wondered briefly if Elizabeth was so perfect that she never even wrinkled the sheets when she slept.

Elizabeth cleared her throat softly. "If there's something you want to talk about—"

"Yeah, actually," Gin-Yung interrupted, anxious to get to the point. "Um, could I come in?"

Shaking her head, Elizabeth pointed to the other bed. Amid a sea of purple sheets, clothes, notebooks, stuffed animals, shoes, and magazines lay a tangle of blond hair that Gin-Yung assumed belonged to Jessica Wakefield.

"Jessica's still sleeping," Elizabeth whispered. "Let's go out to the lounge so we won't wake her."

Gin-Yung had no desire to confront Jessica again. "Fine," she whispered, feeling a little confused. *Has she even talked to Todd yet?* she wondered. *She seems so sad. Then again, maybe she's just feeling guilty at the sight of me.*

Elizabeth grabbed her robe and led Gin-Yung out to the deserted lounge at the end of the hallway in silence. Even though they hadn't seen or spoken to each other since Gin-Yung had returned, there was none of the small talk that Gin-Yung had become so familiar with over the last few days—no *when did you get back*s, no *how was London*s. *No beating around the bush,* Gin-Yung thought uncomfortably. *We both know exactly what—or* who—*brought me here this morning.*

When they reached the lounge, they both sat down on the old, weathered vinyl chairs and stared at each other uneasily for a few moments.

"So," Elizabeth said, shifting restlessly. "Do you want something to drink? The vending machine's right over—"

"No thanks," Gin-Yung interrupted. "I'm not going to stay long."

"OK." Elizabeth looked down at the floor as if she was waiting for Gin-Yung to get the conversation started.

Gin-Yung took a deep breath and dove in. "So have you talked to Todd at all lately?"

"No," she stated flatly.

Surprised, Gin-Yung snapped up straight in her chair. "He didn't call you last night?"

"I don't know—I turned off the ringer last night so I could clean up and get some studying done. Why, was he supposed to call me?" She looked expectant, but Gin-Yung couldn't tell if it was hope or dread that was written on her face.

"Well, after I talked to him last night . . . I just figured he would have called you," Gin-Yung replied, her head pounding. *Darn these stupid headaches*, she thought, rubbing her temples angrily.

"Wha-What happened last night?" Elizabeth asked meekly. Her eyes were brimming with emotion, her hands almost shaking in anticipation.

I know that look, Gin-Yung realized. *I've seen that look in the mirror before. She wants to be with Todd more than anything else in the world*. Elizabeth's pained look was almost heartbreaking, yet at the same time Gin-Yung found it reassuring. It was easy to see how much Elizabeth loved Todd. *They really* do *belong together*, Gin-Yung realized. *Yes, I am doing the right thing*.

"Gin-Yung, is something wrong?" Elizabeth asked hastily. "You look pale."

"No, I'm fine. I'm just trying to find the right words . . . it's not easy for me."

"OK," Elizabeth replied, her brow creasing

with concern. For whom, Gin-Yung couldn't tell.

Unsteadily Gin-Yung smoothed down her bangs, cleared her throat, and began. "Well, um . . . you probably know that Todd and I had a long talk last night. I wanted to come over this morning and let you know exactly how I felt about everything, so there wouldn't be any doubts in your mind. I figured he would have already spoken to you about it, but . . . oh, well, I guess I'll be the one to tell you."

An anxious pair of sea green eyes watched Gin-Yung carefully. She could practically hear them pleading, *Get to the point. Get to the point.*

"Anyhow, since I've been away, things have changed between Todd and me. Lots of things."

Elizabeth looked down at her slippered feet guiltily.

"No—don't do that, Elizabeth. I know all about you and Todd. And I want you to know that I'm OK with it."

"But now that you're back together again—" She leaned forward, running a hand through her long blond hair remorsefully.

"No, no—that's just it. We *aren't* going to be getting back together. We both decided that it would be better if he dated *you*."

"Me?" Elizabeth's eyes widened disbelievingly. "But he loves *you,* Gin-Yung."

"No, he doesn't. That's what we discussed

last night. Todd loves *you*. He always has. And I think he always will."

Suddenly Elizabeth jolted up from her seat and began pacing around the dreary lounge. "This is crazy. You can't imagine how much Todd missed you while you were in London. He was so lonely."

"I don't imagine he's been too lonely with you around," Gin-Yung deadpanned.

Gasping, Elizabeth rushed over and sat in the seat next to her. She laid a hand on her arm gently. "Please—please don't say that. I'm so sorry I came between you two the way I did."

"You didn't come between us at all. We were as far apart as could be already. You two belong together."

"No—it was all a mistake. I felt so awful when I found out that you were back. I hope you'll forgive me. I know how much you two love—"

All of a sudden, from out of nowhere, Gin-Yung felt herself begin to laugh. She laughed so long and hard that she had to put a hand to her sore stomach. "Elizabeth," she began, wiping a tear from her eye, "this is so stupid. Listen to what you're saying. Listen to what *we're* saying."

"What do you mean?" Elizabeth asked mock indignantly, as if she were just grasping the absurdity of their conversation as well. Her blue-green eyes were dancing. "What's so strange about us both wanting to give away the guy we love?" She burst into giggles too, leaning back against her chair and sighing when they both were through.

"Now, I've heard of girls arguing that a boy loves *them* and *only* them," Gin-Yung snickered, "but never the other way around."

"We really do sound ridiculous," Elizabeth agreed.

"Anyway, there's no sense arguing about it. Todd and I aren't in love with each other—he loves you, and I'm glad he does."

"But—"

Gin-Yung smiled and held up her hand. "Look, it's OK for you to get back together with Todd. In fact, it's perfect. You see, I met someone else while I was in London."

"Really?" Elizabeth's face lit up, and she beamed. "That's—that's *great!* I'm so happy for you!"

"He's a soccer player named James. I love him a lot." Gin-Yung paused. Since last night she'd had time to make up a whole profile on her so-called boyfriend—just in case Elizabeth happened to ask what he looked like or what position he played, but Elizabeth didn't ask for any further specifics. Instead she'd fallen for the lie—just as easily as Todd had.

"Anyway," Gin-Yung continued, "that's why

I came by this morning. I'm glad you and Todd are back together, and I don't want to get in the way. In fact, I've always sort of figured you two would patch things up someday."

The tears of joy running down Elizabeth's face made her heart sink. But Gin-Yung pushed her pain aside to stand up and hold out a trembling hand to the winner. "No hard feelings, I hope?"

"Of course not," Elizabeth declared. "Far from it." But instead of shaking Gin-Yung's hand, Elizabeth leaped out of the chair and wrapped her in a suffocating hug. "Thank you, Gin-Yung. Thank you so much," she cried before dashing down the hall. "You don't know what this means to me!"

Yes, I think I do, she replied silently. *Oh, well, if I have to leave Todd with anyone, I'm glad it's going to be you, Elizabeth. Now I don't have to worry about Todd being lonely without me.*

"Take good care of him, Elizabeth," Gin-Yung whispered, her words disappearing into thin air. "Please take good care of my Todd."

Tom felt free and alive as he drove along the coast highway—better than he'd felt in weeks. George's gold Mercedes convertible was a thrill to drive, and with Dana beside him Tom felt like he owned the world.

Besides, who could be depressed with Dana

around? She was a real trip. Her dark curls were caught up in a funky straw hat with huge sunflowers. The flowing scarf she'd tied around her neck flapped behind her like a banner.

"I love convertibles," she said, leaning back and lifting her arms as if to catch the wind.

"Me too. It's a gorgeous day for being in one."

Dana reached over, turned on the radio, and began singing along with it. Tom didn't really agree with her taste in music, but he didn't completely mind it either. He was happy just to see her enjoying herself.

"How was your lesson?" he asked.

"What?" She leaned closer to him. "Sorry, I can't hear you."

"The cello lesson you gave this morning— never mind," Tom said. "It's not important. I was just curious."

"Let's stop if you want to talk awhile," Dana suggested. "There's a public beach right over there."

"Your wish is my command," he joked. Tom followed her directions and whipped the Mercedes into a small roadside parking area.

For an hour Tom sat in the car, enjoying the ocean view, the sunshine on his face, and Dana's chatter. Her stories about her cello students were cracking him up.

"One kid sat me down at the beginning of his

lesson and told me he had a special song to play for me. It turned out to be Led Zeppelin's 'Stairway to Heaven'—which he'd figured out all by himself!"

"Are you kidding?"

"No! It was so funny, I didn't have the heart to stop him. By the time he was finished, we hardly had any time left for an actual lesson."

"At least he was showing some enthusiasm for playing."

"That's for sure. One boy—he was about eight—had a strange habit of breaking his cellos. Or actually 'having little accidents' with them, as his father would describe it."

"What would he do to them?"

"Beats me. One of them looked as if he'd roasted it over a campfire. After the fourth one they finally got the hint and signed their son up for Boy Scouts."

Tom chuckled. "They should have just given him a radio, shown him how to turn it on, and been done with it." He reached over and rubbed Dana's shoulder. "I'm amazed that you can teach kids like that. I don't think I'd have the patience."

"Well, it's a paycheck, for one thing. But then again, it's not always the kids who are the problem. A lot of times it's the parents." Dana shook her head sadly. "They can push their kids awfully hard sometimes."

"Even the ones with no talent?"

"The ones with no talent are usually the ones who are being pushed the hardest." Dana twirled a long mahogany curl thoughtfully around one finger. "I'm afraid a lot of my students are like that. Not your sister, Mary, though. She's so gifted. And self-motivated too. She loves to learn, and I love working with her."

"She thinks a lot of you too."

Dana beamed proudly. "I wish I had started with her when she was younger, but for a ten-year-old she's making unbelievable progress. How about you? Do you play an instrument?"

"Me?" The question took Tom by surprise. "I guess I'm one of those kids who was lucky to be able to play the radio."

With a bell-toned laugh Dana drifted off for a moment and stared out longingly at the beach. "C'mon. I'm tired of sitting here," she said suddenly. "Let's go for a walk." She peeled off her sandals and jumped out of the car.

Tom followed her lead and tucked his shoes under the edge of the seat. "Aren't you worried that your long dress will get dirty?"

"Nope." Dana pulled the scarf from her neck and tied it around her waist. Then she tugged up on her long, gauzy sundress until it ballooned over the scarf. "Voilà, short dress," she declared, striking a pose.

Tom couldn't help but admire Dana for

being so carefree and impulsive as a girlfriend—yet so responsible, talented, and intelligent as a teacher. *She's a million different women in one,* Tom thought. *And I think I love all of them.*

Dana grabbed Tom's hand, breaking his train of thought, and pulled him toward the sparkling ocean. The sand was hot on their bare feet so they began to run, stopping only when they reached the cool wet sand of the surf line. As the water rushed up at their feet Dana giggled, childlike, and threw herself into Tom's arms.

"Isn't this paradise?" she breathed as Tom picked her up and spun her around.

"Could be." Tom leaned in to kiss her up-turned face, but she wriggled away. She kicked up a fan of water, splashing him, and took off running down the beach, her bare feet leaving delicate tracks in the wet sand. He chased after her, leaving his own trail of footprints for the tide to fill.

He had almost caught her when a gust of wind sent her hat flying.

"My hat! Tom, catch it!"

Tom took off after the hat as it tumbled across the sand. It finally came to rest at the very edge of the water. Just when Tom reached for it, a wave crashed over both him and the hat, knocking him to the ground.

"Oh no. My poor hat!" Dana yelled with mock dismay.

"Forget the hat," Tom growled teasingly, catching Dana's leg and pulling her down onto the wet sand beside him.

Dana's giggles turned to indignant squeals when Tom plopped the drenched hat atop her head. Her wide-set hazel eyes twinkled under the dripping brim. Impulsively he pulled her wet body against his and they kissed, playfully at first, and then more passionately until a powerful wave crashed over the top of them, breaking them apart.

"Look at us," Dana sputtered as she crawled out of the surf. "We look like a couple of shipwreck victims."

"*You* don't," Tom assured her, gazing at the soggy curls around her face and the little drops of water caught in her eyelashes. "In fact, you look like a siren. Or a mermaid." Tenderly he pulled her close for another kiss. "And you taste like salt water," he murmured, nuzzling her damp neck.

"I wonder why," she said, kissing Tom's nose before a drop of water dripped off the end of it. She twined her fingers in his hair, firmly but gently. He wanted her to never let go.

Tom felt a tingle of sheer joy shoot up his spine. At that moment Dana was the most beautiful thing Tom had ever seen. Elizabeth's eyes might have been the color of the sea, but Dana's were the color of the sand. Stable, unchanging—he could trust those eyes.

This is what life is all about, he thought as he melted into another lingering kiss. *I have a great new family and a perfect girlfriend. This is as good as it gets.*

Elizabeth didn't think she'd be able to breathe again properly until she found Todd. As soon as she left Gin-Yung in the lounge she ran back to her room and checked her messages. There were three from Todd—all saying that he had great news for her. After getting showered and changed, she rushed straight to his dorm, only to find a note on his door saying that he was at the athletics center.

She made her way to the athletics center by a combination of dancing, skipping, running, and possibly even floating along the sidewalks. Ever since her talk with Gin-Yung, Elizabeth felt as if she were light enough to fly.

When she got to the center, she spotted Todd immediately on the outdoor basketball courts with Bryan Nelson, Winston Egbert, Danny Wyatt, and four other guys she didn't recognize.

Longingly Elizabeth curled the fingers of one hand through the wire fence surrounding the asphalt court and watched. Her heartbeat sped up to an impossibly quick pace when she realized that Todd was bare chested. The sun glistened off the beads of sweat on his broad, tanned shoulders and torso as he dodged and wove around the other players. His damp hair was slicked back off his face, and he reached up and rubbed his sweatband-covered wrist across his forehead. He looked so much more mature than she remembered, so rugged and handsome. And she couldn't believe that he was hers again—all hers.

Elizabeth almost didn't mind that Todd hadn't noticed her yet—she loved to see him play. She watched the muscles in his calves flex as he went in for a layup. When it fell just short of its mark, he grabbed the rebound, circling wide around the players as he took it outside. Just as Todd poised the ball to shoot, his eyes met Elizabeth's, and his face relaxed into an easy smile. Then he looked back toward the basket and let the ball fly from his fingertips in a perfect arch. Elizabeth watched with pride as the ball swished through the basket, touching nothing but net.

"Show-off," Winston yelled.

"I'm taking five, guys," Todd called over his shoulder as he bent down and snatched his shirt off the ground. He used it to wipe the sweat from his face and neck as he jogged out the wire fence door to meet Elizabeth. Back on the court the game resumed without him.

"There you are," Todd said, sounding relieved

and slightly out of breath. He leaned back against the fence. "I was beginning to wonder if you'd left town or something."

"Nope," Elizabeth remarked, wanting desperately to throw herself into his muscular arms and not caring what the other guys would say if she did. "Just turned the ringer off to do some studying."

"That's what I figured." His brown eyes shimmered as he draped the damp T-shirt around his shoulders. "I'm so glad you found me here, Liz. I've got some great news."

"I know," she said, putting her hand on his arm. Even though she'd had plenty of sun, her hand seemed pale in comparison to Todd's bronzed skin.

"You do? How?"

"Gin-Yung came to see me this morning. She told me everything."

Todd's eyebrows shot upward. "Even about her new boyfriend?"

"Mm-hmm. I'm so happy for her."

"Talk about perfect timing. I'm really glad you convinced me to talk to her, Liz. All along there was nothing for us to worry about." Todd ran his hands over his hair, shaking off a few droplets of sweat.

"And she was so happy about the two of us being together—she was practically encouraging it."

"That girl is unbelievable. She's been so cool about this whole thing. She's really gone out of her way for us."

"She's a good person, Todd. We both know that."

"We should thank her."

"Some other day," Elizabeth said, leaning into Todd's warm chest. She wrapped her arms around his neck, tracing her fingers around a few beads of sweat that lingered there. "Today you're all mine."

Todd's grin made her heart soar. "See, I promised I'd come back to you, Liz," he murmured. But just as he was about to lean in for a kiss, he suddenly jerked away.

"Wait—I'm all hot and sweaty. Don't you want me to go back to the dorm and shower first?"

Elizabeth shook her head firmly. "I don't want you to go *anywhere*," she purred, putting her arms back around his neck. As he pulled her into a sweaty embrace she whispered, "I don't want you out of my sight. Not for a long, long time. I love you, Todd Wilkins, sweat and all."

Chapter Eleven

Oh, great! Jessica thought. *Now, on top of every-thing, I've chewed off all my nail polish.* She held out her fingers to inspect the damage. As nervous as she was, it was a wonder she hadn't chewed her nails down to the first knuckle.

Jessica was about to die from suspense—or maybe sheer boredom. She had been waiting outside the police station in the Jeep for fifty-three whole minutes. But she would wait for Nick all night if she had to. Since he was refusing to take her phone calls, catching him as he left work was her only hope of talking to him.

It was after seven when she finally saw him and a couple of other detectives coming out of the side door. They all turned toward the police parking lot.

Jessica jumped from the Jeep and ran toward

him, temporarily forgetting that she had been parked across the street. Brakes squealed, a horn blared, and a driver yelled angrily, but Jessica charged ahead, unscathed.

When she caught up to him, Nick and his fellow officers were gathered next to his black Camaro, talking and laughing. Nick's back was to her. With nothing left to lose, Jessica tapped him on his shoulder.

Nick turned sharply, and as soon as their eyes met, his face turned cold. "What do you want?" he asked rudely.

Jessica cringed, the hate in his eyes overpowering her. "Just to explain," she whispered.

Dub Harrison was in the midst of lighting a cigar when he seemed to catch wind of the situation. "We'll catch you later, Nick," he said with a little too much emphasis.

"No, you guys wait up. This shouldn't take long," Nick replied casually.

Not going to take long? How can he be so inconsiderate? How can he be so foolish? Jessica wondered as her meekness melted away into fierce determination. Pulling her strength back together, she crossed her arms in front of her heatedly. "Don't listen to him, guys. This is going to take as long as *I* say it will."

"Oooh, man. We're gonna cut here, Nick.

Good luck," Dub remarked as he and the others politely and quickly made their exit.

"OK, now that you've driven off my friends," Nick growled, his face reddening, "I'll repeat myself. What do you want?"

"I want to talk to you, Nick. I *need* to talk to you." Now that they were alone, Jessica no longer felt as confident as she had a few moments ago. In fact, she felt absolutely terrified.

"There's nothing to say." Nick's piercing green eyes cut straight to her heart. His perfect face was as rigid as if it had been chiseled from marble.

"Please, Nick. Maybe you don't have anything to say, but I do," she said, hoping her voice didn't sound as shaky as it felt.

"Well, then, let me put it a different way. You have nothing to say that I want to hear."

"How do you know that if you won't at least *listen* to me?" Jessica reached out for his hand, but he waved her off. "Nick, I tried calling you about a hundred times while you were working, but no one would put me through. The one time I got through to you this morning, you hung up on me. Why?"

Nick shrugged as if he thought Jessica were a fool for even asking. "I bet you're not used to that. I'm probably the only one of your many, many boyfriends with enough guts to actually hang up on you."

Jessica held up her hands pleadingly. "But I don't *have* many, many boyfriends. That's what I'm trying to *tell* you."

"Sorry. I guess 'many' is a relative term. How many would you consider *too* many, Jess?"

"Nick, you're the only—"

"Now, I happen to consider more than one to be too many," Nick interrupted. "When I saw you last night, I couldn't believe my eyes."

"I'm really sorry, Nick. I made a big mistake, and I feel horrible about the whole thing. Simply horrible."

"You should. How could you do this to me, Jess? I thought we had something special. I trusted you."

"Please, it's not what you think. I can explain."

"What's to explain? I know what I saw. I have twenty-twenty vision."

"But maybe . . . maybe you didn't see what you thought you saw."

"Jessica, so help me, if you try to tell me I saw your twin sister, I'm going to have you locked up. I can tell the two of you apart a mile away!"

"No, you didn't see Elizabeth." Jessica looked down dejectedly and stared at a cigarette butt that had been ground into the gravel. "It was me."

"Damn right it was you. You were center stage at Marvioso, dressed to kill, and cheating on me."

"No, Nick." Jessica's face shot up, her eyes pleading with all the strength she could muster. "I wasn't cheating on you. I would never do that to you. I love you."

"I don't think you know what the word *love* means, Jess."

"Yes, I do. It's what I feel for you. You're the best thing that's happened to me in years, Nick. I thought you knew that."

Nick's face softened slightly for a second, and he almost seemed to move toward her, but then he backed off and stiffened his jaw. "OK, Jess, I'll listen. Let me guess—that guy was your cousin from out of town, right?"

"No, it was Bobby Hornet, the singer. He's choosing the models for the calendar I told you about. The calendar that you really wanted me to be in."

"Oh, Bobby Hornet. Of *course*."

Her heart plummeting, Jessica launched into her defense. "No, Nick, you just don't get it. Bobby was thinking about choosing me for the spot, so he asked me out to dinner, and I agreed. And that's *all* it was—dinner, nothing else. Even then I felt so guilty about being seen with another guy that I couldn't even eat. In fact, right before you drove by, I'd just finished telling him to forget the whole thing. I told him I didn't want to be in the calendar—that a stupid dinner with him wasn't even worth it."

Nick's dark brows creased. "But—but I thought you were desperate to be in that calendar."

"I was, but not if it meant losing you. You mean more to me than any dumb modeling job ever could."

"You'd really give up your chance to be in the calendar for me?" As if he were finally understanding the situation, the tenseness in Nick's jaw seemed to disappear, and his gaze grew softer.

Jessica stepped forward and put her hands on Nick's waist. He didn't pull away. "I'd do anything for you. You know that," she said quietly as she felt the hot sting of tears come to her eyes. "I don't want to lose you, Nick. Not over something like this."

Nick slumped back against his car and ran his hand along the stubble on his chin. He said nothing.

"Nick, please understand," Jessica pleaded urgently. "It was all a big mistake. Can't you forgive me?"

To Jessica's relief, Nick's scowl gave way to a sad smile. "Oh, Jess. Why can't I ever stay mad at you?" he asked, the corners of his eyes crinkling.

He reached out and pulled Jessica into his arms for a hug that nearly took her breath away.

"Don't scare me like that ever again," he whispered into her baby-soft hair. "I hated thinking that you were with someone else. I love you so much. Too much, in fact."

Jessica beamed into his shoulder. "I love you too." When Nick loosened his grip, she turned to look up at him squarely. "And believe me, I really do know what that means."

He tucked a strand of hair behind her ear. "That sure was some dress!" he said with a boyish grin, his eyes twinkling. "Will you wear it for me sometime?"

"We can go get it right now, if you want," she murmured. "But after that awful night, I don't think I ever want to put it on again."

As Nick pulled her in for a rapturous kiss all the guilt Jessica had been feeling vanished in an instant. She was grateful to have Nick's arms holding her safe and close to him, because she felt as if she could practically drift away from all the weight being lifted off her shoulders. *Guilt! Ick!* she thought as she pressed her lips to his. *The world would be a much better place without it.*

"Do you want to come inside?" Dana whispered as Tom pulled the Mercedes over to the curb in front of her rented house.

"I'd love to, but I can't," Tom replied regretfully.

Dana stuck out her bottom lip and toyed with her tattered straw hat. "Are you in a big hurry to get rid of me?"

"Not at all."

"Well, come on in. You can meet my roommates."

"As appealing as that offer is, I really have to go."

"All right, you don't have to meet my roommates. We can watch the late movie and get cozy on the couch."

"Now, that *definitely* sounds appealing, but I can't. It's getting late, and I have to get the car back—"

Dana interrupted him with a kiss that made it hard for him to keep saying no.

"I *really* have to go," Tom gasped, breaking away reluctantly.

With an exaggerated scowl Dana got out of the car and slammed the door.

"Come here, you crazy girl."

Dana flounced around to the driver's side and leaned over the door for another embrace. When they parted, Dana's gaze smoldered seductively.

Tom leaned back in the leather seat and moaned. "I told you, I've got to take this car back to George's. It'll be way past your bedtime when I get back to campus."

"Want me to come with you?"

"I thought you said you had an early class tomorrow."

"I do, but—oh, all right, I'm going, since you're so *anxious* to get rid of me."

He pressed his lips to hers hard enough to convince her he had absolutely no desire to be rid of her whatsoever.

Seemingly satisfied, Dana stepped away from the car and blew him a kiss before she spun around and ran into the house.

As Tom pulled away from the curb he let out a contented yawn. The day had been absolutely flawless. *Dana might be a bit of a tease,* he thought, *but she's exciting, loving, and more full of life than anyone I've ever met. She's everything I need right now—and maybe, just maybe, for a long time to come.*

Before he pulled onto the freeway, he considered putting the top up, but the black, starry sky was so dazzling, and the wind in his face so invigorating, he decided to leave it down. He wanted to stretch the glory of the day as long as he could.

Once Tom reached the Conroy condo, he parked the Mercedes in the garage, took the elevator up to the private entrance, and let himself in. The entryway was dark, and with the wide vertical blinds shutting out both the sights and the sound of the city, the condo seemed eerily vacant. *George and the kids must still be at the movies,* he figured as the glow from a single brass lamp in the sunken living room provided him with enough light to make his way down the hall.

Turning to the left, he clicked on the kitchen light and dropped the car keys onto the kitchen table. The white-on-white, spotless room seemed sterile and empty, but Tom remembered how it had been last night when the four of them had scarfed down two huge pizzas after George's health-food fiasco. Even though the dinner had gotten off to an uncomfortable start, the whole evening had turned out to be great—and Tom's calling Mr. Conroy "Dad" for the first time had been the icing on the cake.

Speaking of cake—I wonder if there's any left, Tom thought, recalling the amazing triple-layer devil's food cake that his father had been hiding in the fridge for dessert. Tom peeked into the refrigerator, took out the cake, and cut himself a slice. Then he poured a tall glass of milk and sat at the table to enjoy his late-night snack.

While he was eating, he stared at the ring of keys on the table. They seemed blatantly out of place in the neat room. Since George had been gracious enough to lend him the convertible, the least Tom could do would be to put the keys back in their proper place—in that rolltop desk in George's study. Tom finished off his snack, set the dishes carefully in the sink, and, key ring in hand, headed for the study.

Tom clicked on the stained-glass desk lamp and rolled open the heavy desktop. What he saw surprised him. The inside of the desk was cluttered and messy, and Tom knew that Mr. Conroy was obsessively neat. *He's even worse than Eliz—* He cut off the thought, still savoring the tingle of Dana's good-night kisses on his lips.

Tom dropped the keys into a marble tray that held other keys, but as he reached out to roll the desktop closed again he noticed a picture of himself—with Elizabeth Wakefield. His first shocked impulse was to jerk it up and rip it to pieces, but he liked to think he was beyond throwing temper tantrums just because something reminded him of that girl he used to date.

It's only natural for George to want a picture of me, he reasoned. *After all, I was the one who gave George the picture, and pretty much all recent pictures of me have her in there somewhere too.*

Tom picked up the picture gingerly, as if it might grow teeth and bite him. And in a way it did, for all the pain it caused him. In the picture he was looking at the camera, but Elizabeth was staring up into his face. *She looks so loving,* he

217

thought bitterly. *What an act!* Almost against his will a wave of nausea swept over him. *I guess it really* is *over between us—forever,* he realized with crushing finality.

Sighing, Tom flipped the photograph over and over in his hands and traced the edges with his fingertips. *How can I move on with my life when there are reminders of her everywhere?* Tom wondered. Fighting back tears, he made a resolution. *As soon as I get back to campus I'm going to find some better pictures of myself—pictures without this woman in them.*

Tom tossed the picture back into the desk angrily, but it didn't look right. Knowing Mr. Conroy, there was probably some sort of organization even amid the clutter. Tom looked over the desk's contents, trying to remember where the picture had been so he could leave everything exactly the way he'd found it.

"Wait, what's this?" he whispered aloud to himself. It was another snapshot, again of himself and Elizabeth. His arm was around her shoulders and a wisp of her blond hair was in his face. He remembered the night that picture had been taken. They had seemed so happy then. But that was the night George had taken them out for a celebration at Andre's—the night Elizabeth claimed George had given her an expensive necklace and tried to kiss her.

Tom threw the picture down in disgust.

Beneath that picture was a whole stack of photographs, facedown. Tom didn't want to pry, but his respect for Mr. Conroy's privacy was quickly overridden by his well-developed sense of curiosity. Like a blackjack dealer with a deck of cards, Tom carefully began to turn the pictures over.

. . . a Polaroid shot of himself and Elizabeth the night of his twenty-first birthday party—the very night he'd learned that George was his father.

. . . a Polaroid of George and Elizabeth outside Andre's. Tom had taken the photo himself. *How could she have abused the trust of such a caring, honest man?* he wondered angrily.

. . . a Polaroid of Tom and Elizabeth in front of WSVU, taken that very same night. But it wasn't a very good picture. Tom's face was chopped off from the nose up. He was surprised his father would have bothered to save it.

. . . a newspaper photo of himself and Elizabeth, taken after they had done a major story revealing the basketball point-shaving scandal.

Tom put down the stack of pictures and ran his hand over his face. This was way too painful. Why was he putting himself through such misery? Why couldn't he forget about the pictures and go home?

But he couldn't help himself. Taking a deep

breath, he turned over the next picture.

. . . another newspaper shot—this time just of Elizabeth, when she'd reported on sex discrimination at Kitty's Restaurant.

Where in the world did George get that? Tom wondered. *This happened long before George knew either of us. Surely it wasn't mixed in with the pictures I gave him.*

. . . Elizabeth in a publicity shot for WSVU.

. . . Elizabeth in a newspaper clipping from when she was almost killed by William White.

. . . Elizabeth in front of the courthouse after Jessica's trial.

Tom began turning over the pictures faster. Some of them were pictures he'd never seen, and all of them were of Elizabeth—only Elizabeth. His jaw tightened, and the nauseous feeling in his stomach intensified as he forced himself to keep going.

. . . Elizabeth in a bikini, sunbathing behind Dickenson Hall.

. . . Elizabeth coming out of the library, her arms full of books.

. . . Elizabeth in the parking lot of the Organic Palace.

. . . Elizabeth framed perfectly in her dorm-room window, crying.

These were candid photographs that even Elizabeth couldn't have known were being taken. Dozens of them. Tom's heart clenched. He'd had enough journalistic experience to know that these pictures had all been taken with a telephoto lens, as if the photographer didn't want to be discovered. Some were grainy and out of focus, as if they'd been taken in a hurry.

Bewildered, Tom shuffled through the stack again. So many pictures of Elizabeth—in Polaroid photos, yellowed newspaper clippings, photocopies of articles, and even an old year-book picture. *Why would George have these?* he asked himself. *Unless*—

The truth hit him like a punch to the stomach.

Chapter
Twelve

_____

"Jessica, we thought you'd never get here!" Isabella Ricci cried, grabbing Jessica's arm and rushing her through the crowded Theta lounge. "What took you so long?"

"I couldn't find a thing to wear," Jessica said offhandedly. It seemed a believable excuse, but actually Jessica had dawdled all morning. She couldn't see much sense in rushing across campus just to hear Bobby Hornet announce that he had decided to let some other, more "deserving" girl represent Theta Alpha Theta in the charity calendar. And the worst of it was that it would probably be Alison Quinn, of all people.

Oh, well, at least I'm back with Nick, she assured herself. _That's really all that matters._ Her concentration was broken as she felt the stare of a couple of nearby Theta pledges on her.

"Look, there's Jessica," she heard one of them say. "She's the one who wore that bikini to Disc-Oh! Music."

"I guess she's pretty sure she'll get picked, huh?" her friend whispered, none too softly.

Infuriated, Jessica glared at them until they slunk away to safety among the other pledges. *You don't know as much as you* think *you know,* Jessica said silently. She hadn't told anyone except Lila, Isabella, Elizabeth, and of course Nick that she'd run off like Cinderella at midnight, leaving Bobby Hornet holding a marinated mushroom instead of a glass slipper. They were the only ones who knew she didn't have a snowball's chance of getting selected now.

She sighed as the quiet murmurs in the room were broken by an announcement from Kimberly Schyler, the Theta treasurer. "Well, enjoy the refreshments, girls," she declared sarcastically. "Thanks to Celine Bordreaux, you'll be eating the last of our entertainment budget until the next fund-raiser."

"And such fine refreshments they are!" Lila sneered, dipping a limp carrot stick into a greenish dressing after Kimberly walked away.

"Has anyone seen Bobby yet?" Tina Chai asked breathlessly as she rushed up to the table.

"No!" everyone said in unison. "Not yet."

As much as Jessica despised Tina Chai, she

almost wished she could be feeling some of the excitement that shone in her eyes. "Oh, what does it matter anyway," she muttered bitterly, not even realizing she'd spoken out loud.

"That's right, Jess. What does it matter?" Lila chirped up. "The calendar will probably be a major bomb. I mean, no one's going to want to buy it if all the models look like Alison."

"Ecch." Isabella crinkled up her perfect nose. "What a horrifying thought."

"Look, I'm going to go find us a seat," Lila said. "No telling how long this will take with Alison in charge."

"And I'll get us something to drink," Isabella said. She popped open a can of diet cola and poured it into three small paper cups.

Jessica helped carry the drinks over to the couch that Lila had claimed for them. Whether or not it had been empty before Lila got there, Jessica didn't ask. She knew that Lila was an expert at pushing her weight around.

"*Très chic,*" Lila said when Isabella handed her the paper cup. "I guess we should be grateful we're not sipping tap water right from the sink."

"Shall we toast?" Isabella said, holding her paper cup in the air. "To the calendar."

"No, not to the stupid calendar," Jessica said. "I can't believe that's all anybody is talking about." She drained her soda in one gulp and flopped down on the couch between Isabella and Lila. "I'll bet it's going to be really tacky—probably just cheap, blurry black-and-white pictures taken by one of the kids from the yearbook staff."

"Right," Lila offered. "It'll probably look like one of those cheesy calendars you get for free when you open a bank account."

"Did I hear the word *cheesy?*" Denise Waters asked as she flopped down on the floor in front of the couch. "You couldn't possibly be describing our reception for Bobby Hornet, could you? I mean, look at the glorious spread we've laid out for him."

"We know," Jessica replied grumpily, her spirits hardly lifted by her friends' displays of solidarity.

"C'mon, Jessica, lighten up," Isabella said.

"Yeah, you win a few, you lose a few," Lila added.

Easy for you to say, she growled silently as she snatched up the latest issue of *Fashion Forward* and began to idly flip through its pages.

Isabella and Lila continued to carry on a conversation right over her head, as if she weren't there. Jessica *hated* to be ignored.

"Calendar, calendar, calendar. Why is everyone so wrapped up in this stupid calendar thing?" Jessica interrupted.

"Admit it, Jess. You're here for the same reason

everyone else is—to hear Bobby's announcement."

"No, I'm not. I don't care who he chooses. I'm just here to hang out with you guys."

Suddenly the room went silent. Jessica looked up from her magazine to see Alison Quinn, her hair painstakingly arranged and her makeup far too elaborate for a Monday morning. She did her little half clap and shrilled, "Everyone, listen up. Your attention, please!"

When Alison cleared her throat, Jessica sank lower into the sofa. *Oh no,* she thought. Please, *don't make a speech.*

Her prayers were answered, sort of. Alison didn't make a speech, but when Bobby Hornet stepped up to the makeshift podium, he began to.

Jessica couldn't bear to look him in the face as he began speaking. She alternately flipped magazine pages, stared at her fingernails, or whispered to Isabella and Lila. She only caught bits and pieces of what he was saying.

". . . I hope you realize what a service we will be doing with this calendar. As you know, I gave ten percent of the profits of my last CD to the Sweet Valley homeless shelter, but there is still so much to do. . . ."

Jessica looked around the room. She couldn't believe how everyone was soaking up his every word. The place was as quiet as a church.

". . . and no one can deny the eternal lure of the female form in all its beauty. The pictures of the beautiful young woman I've chosen to represent Theta Alpha Theta will sell hundreds of calendars and put food on the plates of just as many hungry men, women, and children. . . ."

Hmmm, now I like that a lot, Jessica thought, her eyes glued to the magazine pages. *Of course, if it came in a nice solid pink instead of that garish zebra pattern, I might actually wear it. As for those shoes, however—*

"Pay *attention*, Jess," Lila hissed. "Bobby's going to announce the winner any second."

"Good," Jessica whispered back. "Maybe by the time Alison's name is called, I might actually have my next season's wardrobe planned out."

". . . and last but not least, you ladies of Theta Alpha Theta should be proud to hear that your organization will not only be represented in the December layout but also on the calendar cover. Let's give Jessica Wakefield and all the Theta women a big hand."

Nope, those shoes have got to go. Maybe a nice stack-heel pump, but not too high—

"Jess!" Isabella broke into her mental shopping spree, shaking her arm violently. "Jessica, he said *you!*"

"Me?" Jessica shot up straight in the saggy couch and dropped the magazine to the floor. "I won?"

"You won, already!" Lila said proudly, trying to push Jessica off the couch. "Now why don't you go up there and do something about it?"

"Me?" Jessica repeated in shock as she walked up to Bobby Hornet in such a daze, she could hardly notice the applause. When she reached the podium, Bobby gave her hand a vigorous shake while a photographer from the *Sweet Valley Gazette* snapped a picture.

As Alison stepped up to the podium to make some closing announcements Bobby took Jessica by the arm gently and led her out into the hallway.

"I can't believe you actually *chose* me!" she exclaimed after she finally caught her breath. "How could you, after Saturday night?"

"Miss Scarlet, surely you didn't think that dating me was a requirement for modeling in the calendar," Bobby drawled casually.

"Uh, no, of course not," Jessica lied. "Why would I think *that*?"

"You tell me, Jessica. Somehow I got that idea." As he laughed Alison suddenly came out in the hallway and scooted in between them. "As a matter of fact," he began as he slipped an arm around Alison's waist, "Alison and I are going out tonight."

"That's right." Alison smiled possessively. "No hard feelings, Jessica. You'll be perfect for the calendar. As Bobby says, they were looking for the California surfer-girl type," she explained. "I'm much more *European* looking."

"Wow! What a slam to Europeans," Isabella whispered as she snuck up behind Jessica and gave her a congratulatory hug.

Jessica sighed deeply, finally able to take it all in. She did it—she was going to be a model! She couldn't wait to tell Nick.

"Way to go, Jess!" Lila cheered as Jessica walked back into the lounge.

"Yeah! Let's hear it!" Denise called as the Thetas all applauded once again—and this time Jessica was actually conscious enough to hear it.

"And by the way," Lila whispered, putting her arm around Jessica's shoulders, "just forget everything I said before about the calendar. I'm sure it's going to be fabulous."

Suddenly Lila's eyes widened, and Jessica followed her gaze to see Bobby Hornet standing on her other side.

"Bobby, this is my best friend, Lila—"

"Charmed." Lila shook Bobby's hand quickly and daintily. "Um, I'll just leave you two alone, OK?" she said with a low giggle before she hurried away.

Clearing her throat, Jessica looked around the lounge furtively. After all that had happened, the last thing she wanted was Alison getting on her case for talking to "her" man. "Um, Bobby, I just want to thank you for—"

"The pleasure is all mine, Jessica," Bobby interrupted. "But I wish you had told me your boyfriend was Nick Fox."

Jessica had thought that nothing else could surprise her this morning, but she'd just been proven wrong. She felt as if her jaw had dropped all the way down to the vine-patterned carpeting. "*You* know *Nick?*"

"Sure. He came to see me at the hotel last night. He's a great guy. In fact, my brother Reggie is in his precinct! You should say hi to him next time you're there. Reggie's younger and more pumped than I am, but we look a lot alike."

Suddenly Jessica remembered the gorgeous cop she'd seen when she brought Nick lunch last week; she'd noticed the similarity even then. "I have a feeling I've seen him before," she said with a sly smile.

"Well, I know you're beautiful and all, but after I found out you were dating Nick Fox, how could I *not* choose you?" Bobby winked. "Just kidding, Jess. I knew you were perfect for the calendar from the second I saw you." He squeezed her arm amiably. "Ciao."

Jessica sighed in amazement as she watched Bobby walk away. Nick visited Bobby Hornet last night? *Unbelievable*. Jessica made a mental note to ask Lila if she could keep the red dress for one more night. She wanted to thank Nick in a way he'd never forget.

"Lila." Jessica grabbed her best friend's arm as she sauntered by. "Did I ever tell you that I have the best boyfriend in the whole world?"

"Why, yes, Jessica." Lila groaned, rolling her eyes. "I believe you might have mentioned that about a million times."

"Well, then, let's make it a million and one. *I have the best boyfriend in the whole world!*"

Todd rubbed his hands roughly over his face. He was exhausted. As if his string of Monday classes weren't bad enough, Coach Falk had kept the team after basketball practice to run laps. Now he was standing in front of Gin-Yung's house—and he was late.

He'd told Gin-Yung he'd show up around five-thirty to return a few things she'd left in his dorm room back before she went to London. He glanced at his watch and winced. It was now six forty-five.

She's going to think I've turned into an unreliable bum, he thought. After ringing the doorbell, he looked in the shopping bag at Gin-Yung's things. He doubted it was anything she'd miss—a couple of books, a CD, and an SVU sweatshirt—but it made a convenient excuse for coming over.

If he'd told Gin-Yung his real reason for coming when he called, she probably would have told him she was busy. She always hated gushy emotional scenes.

Well, she might not want to hear it, but I've got to tell her how wonderful I think she is. Her going to see Elizabeth yesterday morning was one of the most unselfish, thoughtful, and bravest things anyone had ever done. She could have stayed away and let things progress on their own, but that wasn't Gin-Yung's way. It was hard for Todd to believe that she could be so concerned about Elizabeth's feelings, especially when her own long-distance relationship with the soccer player was up in the air.

Maybe Gin-Yung and her boyfriend will work something out, Todd thought. *I hope so. Gin-Yung deserves to be happy. But why isn't she coming to the door?*

He rang the bell again and waited. Nothing. He knew the doorbell was working; he could hear it echoing softly inside the house. But he knocked, just to be on the safe side. Still no one answered. He backed away from the porch and peeked in the living-room window. There were lights on inside, and he could hear a television— the nightly news was on.

Todd was confused. When he'd called earlier, Gin-Yung had assured him she would be home all evening. "I'm not going anywhere," had been her exact words. *Did she get angry at me for being late?* he wondered. *No, Gin-Yung wouldn't do something like that.*

Frustrated, Todd leaned on the bell for a good fifteen seconds. He was about to give up when the door popped open.

Todd gasped at what he saw. For a second he thought he was looking at an old woman . . . but it was Gin-Yung. Her normally toasted-almond skin was as white as wet chalk. Her eyes were swollen shut and circled with deep, dark shadows. Her mouth was pinched and bluish. She leaned against the door frame, looking as if she was barely able to stand.

"Gin-Yung! What's wrong?"

"Oh, Todd," Gin-Yung murmured. She held out her hands as if she were fumbling through a dark room. "I was so scared—"

"Who else is here? Are you all alone?"

"They're gone . . . I was alone . . . so scared . . ."

With those words she pitched forward and collapsed. Todd dropped her belongings and managed to grab her just before she hit the ground.

"Gin, have you taken something?" He knelt with her head cradled in his arms and patted her pale cheeks gently. She felt cold—deathly cold. "Wake up, please! Talk to me!" But she didn't move.

"Help!" Todd shouted hoarsely, looking around frantically to see if any neighbors were nearby. "Someone, please, *help us!*"

But no one was around; no one answered his cries. Not wanting to leave her but knowing he had to, he gently eased Gin-Yung's head to the ground. She shivered violently.

"Help! Please!" he cried one final time before he grabbed the sweatshirt from the bag and draped it over Gin-Yung's convulsing body. Then he rushed inside to call 911.

Elizabeth burst from the hospital elevator in a run, dodging a mop bucket and a yellow placard that read Caution: Wet Floors in three languages. She wouldn't stop until she reached the intensive care unit.

She kept running until she saw Todd in a bleak waiting area at the end of the hall. *He isn't bleeding or bandaged,* she thought. *He's standing. He has to be all right. Oh, please, let Todd be OK.* She dashed straight into his arms. As he held her she could feel his whole body trembling.

"Are you all right?" she asked breathlessly. "I came as soon as you called."

"Oh, Liz, thank goodness you're here. I was about to go crazy."

"*You* were! When you called and said, 'I'm at the hospital, come quick,' and hung up, *I* was

234

the one going crazy! I had no idea what'd happened to you."

"It's not me. It's Gin-Yung."

Elizabeth was startled. "What happened?"

"I'd stopped by her house, and when she answered the door, she looked horrible. Then she just collapsed."

"What caused it? Do you have any idea?"

"No, the doctors haven't told me a thing. I've been pacing up and down this waiting room since we got here. I—I feel so guilty. I wanted to help her, but there was nothing I could do. She just lay there, Liz. She looked *dead!*"

The intense panic in his voice frightened Elizabeth more than the words themselves.

She led Todd to a bench and helped him sit down. She was concerned about what might have happened to Gin-Yung, but at the moment her biggest worry was for her boyfriend. He looked as if he might collapse himself. She sat down beside him and wrapped her arms around his quaking shoulders.

"I was so scared," he whispered. "I tried not to panic, but—"

"It's OK. You got her here," she assured him, putting her cool hands on his flushed cheeks. "She's going to be all right. You'll see."

The sound of running steps on the linoleum distracted her. She turned to see Kim-Mi and

Mrs. Suh speeding down the corridor.

"Where is she?" Mrs. Suh demanded, her voice sounding impossibly high-pitched. "Where's Gin-Yung? I have to see her."

Todd stood up and walked over to meet the petite, older woman at the edge of the waiting area. "They won't let anyone in. The doctor said she would come out and let us know what's going on."

"We should have stayed home with her, Kim! We should *never* have left her alone!" Mrs. Suh cried in anguish. Then she burst into tears. "I must see my baby." She pushed Todd aside and charged toward the double doors to the ICU.

Todd stayed rooted in place, but Kim caught Mrs. Suh, grasping her firmly by the arms and helping her to a nearby chair.

"Mother, we have to wait," she said calmly. "And while we're waiting, you might as well pull yourself together. You know how much Gin hates tears. You can't let her see you going to pieces like this."

"She kept saying she felt fine. We shouldn't have listened to her!" Mrs. Suh dug into her purse and took out a delicate lacy handkerchief. She dabbed at her eyes. Gin-Yung's mother had finally quieted down for the time being, but Elizabeth could see that her flow of tears hadn't slowed any.

Kim straightened up and glared at Todd as if they were gunfighters in a Mexican standoff. "I'm awfully surprised to see *you* here," she spat.

Warily Elizabeth walked over to Todd's side and took his hand. "Kim, is there something wrong with Gin-Yung? Something we should know about?"

"As if you two care!"

"Of *course* we care," Elizabeth said, shocked at the venom in Kim's voice. "Gin-Yung is our friend."

"Has this happened before?" Todd asked hurriedly. "Has Gin-Yung been sick?"

Kim nodded, and tears began to form in her eyes. The simple question broke her down completely. "Yes," she whispered softly, her lips barely moving.

"I should have known something was wrong." Todd clenched his hands into anxious fists. "Every time I spoke to her, she mentioned feeling tired."

"Then why didn't she say anything more?" Elizabeth asked.

"I begged her to tell Todd, but she refused," Kim said. "She wanted to do things her way."

Todd dropped his head. "I should have known anyway," he mumbled. "I should have said something—or asked something. But I was afraid of offending her. I could see she'd lost weight. And she had those dark circles under her eyes. I didn't think it was anything serious."

Elizabeth nervously slipped her arm around Todd's waist. "Kim, what is it? Please tell us."

"She . . . she has a brain tumor," Kim said.

Elizabeth gasped, her hand flying to her face in shock.

"B-But she'll be OK, won't she? With surgery?" Todd asked hopefully. "They can cure those things nowadays, can't they?"

Kim shook her head sadly, tears streaming down her face. "It's inoperable. The doctors in England said Gin-Yung doesn't have long to live. She came back from London just to say . . ." She choked on a sob. "Just to say . . . good-bye."

Elizabeth reeled from the news. "No. Oh no," she murmured, clinging to Todd's arm for support. *Oh, Gin-Yung,* she thought, *I'm sorry. I'm so very, very sorry.*

Her eyes flooding with tears, Elizabeth looked up at Todd, hoping to find strength in his eyes. But his brown eyes were filled only with crushing sadness. He said nothing as a single tear rolled slowly down his cheek and dropped onto Elizabeth's blouse.

Don't miss Sweet Valley University #29, <u>One Last Kiss.</u> Here's a sneak peek!

We can't think of ourselves right now, Todd. We have to do whatever's best for Gin-Yung. Elizabeth's words echoed in Todd's ears as he stood timidly in the middle of the hallway. What if the doctor *was* right? What if Gin-Yung really was dying? Todd sucked in a sharp breath, keeping a rise of panic at bay.

But Todd had to see her first. He had to know the truth.

With a slow, reluctant turn Todd headed toward the long white corridor of the intensive care unit, moving one foot stiffly in front of the other. His head pounded in fierce, hammering blows. With cold, shaking fingers he kneaded the tension in his brow, his eyes fixed on the scrubbed white floor tiles. *What am I going to say to Gin-Yung when I see her?* he wondered.

What do you say to someone you know is dying? Todd continued to stare at the floor ahead of him, not daring to look into the open doors of the other intensive care rooms he passed. The hall was ominously silent except for the squeak of Todd's basketball sneakers as he trudged apprehensively toward Gin-Yung's room.

When he reached ICU room number six, Todd turned his toes toward the door and walked in, eyes still grazing the floor. The room was dark except for a dim fluorescent light coming from somewhere on the far side. Todd stopped in the doorway, slowly lifting his gaze from the floor to the chrome wheels of the hospital bed up to the orange blanket covering Gin-Yung's thin legs. Todd's frightened heart thundered as he watched the shallow rise and fall of Gin-Yung's chest. She was obviously having trouble breathing.

Swallowing hard, Todd summoned his courage enough to move his eyes over until they finally came to rest on Gin-Yung's thin, sallow face. Her glossy, blue-black hair was gone, replaced by a pale, grayish cap of stubble. Her sunken cheeks and closed eyes showed no trace of the healthy glow Gin-Yung used to have. She didn't look like the same person at all.

Todd looked up at the room number one more time just to be sure. *Number six.* He fell against the door and reached for the knob to steady himself. The emotions he'd locked tightly away were screaming to get out. *It's true,* Todd thought, his lips quivering. *It really is true.*

"What are they doing to you?" he whispered, glaring at the tangled maze of tubes surrounding her. Skinny IV tubes were taped to Gin-Yung's right arm, feeding a clear liquid directly into her veins. A wider respirator tube was coming out of her mouth, while two smaller tubes pumped oxygen into her nose. Wires were taped to her head and chest, leading to the various monitors that beeped and hummed around her. And yet through all of this Gin-Yung lay completely still and silent.

I can't believe this is happening to you, Gin. It's so unfair. Tears suddenly sprang to Todd's eyes as he watched Gin-Yung breathe, the harsh light above the bed giving her skin a strange, otherworldly glow. He imagined himself lying there, surrounded by equipment, struggling to fill his own lungs with air, knowing he was going to die. Involuntarily a terrified sob wrenched out of his throat.

As if she heard him, Gin-Yung blinked slowly a few times, her dark, almond-shaped eyes opening a fraction. She stared at Todd under half-closed lids, blankly at first. After a few moments a tiny smile tugged around the thick white respirator tube.

Todd's fingers gripped the handle of the doorknob tightly. "Hi . . . Gin," he muttered, finding it hard to connect that name with the shadow of a person who lay there.

With frail fingers Gin-Yung pulled aside the respirator, her colorless lips curving into a weak smile. "Oh, Todd," she whispered hollowly. "Come closer . . . I can hardly see you."

Todd edged nearer, arms moving woodenly at his sides. A steady stream of salty tears trickled down his face as he stopped at the foot of the bed. He was afraid to get any closer to the delicate network of tubes and machines surrounding her, as if his very presence might cause them to break down.

But when Todd's sad eyes met hers, he recognized the faintest spark of the fire that had once burned so brightly there. "Oh, Gin-Yung . . ." Todd's voice broke as he gingerly placed his hand on her bony ankle. Even through the blanket it felt cold. "I don't know what to say—"

"You don't have to say anything," Gin-Yung interrupted in a raspy voice. Her red-rimmed eyes were damp.

Todd looked down. "Why did you keep this from me?"

"It's not that I didn't want you to know. . . ." She stopped to take a raspy breath. "I just couldn't find the strength to tell you."

"I could've helped you through this," Todd blurted almost mechanically, unsure if he really could have been of any help to Gin-Yung at all. But it seemed like the right thing to say at the moment.

"I know," Gin-Yung murmured, gently wiggling her foot against his hand. "But you're here now. That's what matters."

An awkward silence fell between them. What was Gin-Yung expecting from him? Was it more than he was willing to give? Todd wiped his face with his shirtsleeve, feeling burdened by the sudden responsibility and terrified that he was going to fail miserably.

"I'm so sorry, Gin-Yung," Todd choked, not knowing what else to say. "I'm just so *sorry*."

"Don't you dare make me cry, Todd Wilkins," Gin-Yung ordered, her thin voice wavering. "It hurts too much."

"Not *again!*" Elizabeth rooted through her leather backpack, hoping to find her blue Restoration poetry textbook. But her thick French book was there in its place. "I can't believe I've done this *twice* today," she mumbled tiredly to herself before she spun around on her sandaled heels and marched out of the austere English building. The thought of trekking all the way across campus again filled her with dread. She only had five minutes to rush back to her room and get the right book before class started.

I just can't concentrate on anything lately.

Elizabeth popped on a denim baseball cap and adjusted the visor to shield her eyes from the bright midday sun. She seemed to be moving in slow motion, as if she were walking through water. The baggy denim overalls she was wearing swished around her ankles as she walked. Why did her dorm seem so far away today? She'd never reach it and get back to class in time.

"Liz, wait up!"

Elizabeth looked up to see Todd rushing toward her. He was wearing the same rugby shirt and jeans as the day before. *Please tell me you're coming to take me away to a deserted island,* Elizabeth pleaded silently.

"Oh, Todd," Elizabeth breathed at the sight of his downcast face. He looked as if he'd aged overnight. "How is Gin-Yung?" she asked, tenderly touching the stubble on his chin.

"As well as can be expected," Todd answered heavily. His soft brown eyes stared at her for a moment, then he leaned toward Elizabeth and pressed his lips to hers in a slow, lingering kiss.

Elizabeth closed her eyes and breathed in Todd's warmth, hoping the kiss would never end. She wrapped her arms around his neck, feeling Todd's strong arms encircling her waist. They fit together so comfortably, so perfectly.

Yet in the middle of her moment of bliss the

memory of Gin-Yung nagged at the back of Elizabeth's mind. Feelings of guilt slipped in and out of her consciousness lightly and more easily than Elizabeth had expected. One minute she was thinking of Gin-Yung, and a moment later the sensation of Todd's lips on the hollow of her throat made her forget everything.

Todd pulled away slightly, his arms still wrapped around her. His eyelids drooped. "It was awful seeing her, Liz," he said hoarsely. "I almost didn't recognize her. There are all these machines and tubes . . . and she's so weak. . . ."

Elizabeth's heart became heavy again. "Is she conscious?"

"She slides in and out of it," he said. "I talked to her a little."

Looking down, Elizabeth placed her palms flat against Todd's chest. "Is she scared?"

Todd nodded, parting his lips to speak but faltering before he could. Elizabeth rested her head on his chest and felt Todd's strong, clear heartbeat pound against her cheek. *We have so much more time ahead of us*, Elizabeth thought. *And Gin-Yung has none.*

"She lied about having a boyfriend, Liz," Todd whispered.

Elizabeth looked up at him uncomprehendingly. "What?"

Todd pressed his chin against her forehead.

"She made him up so you and I could stay together. She said she wanted to leave me with you."

"Oh, Todd!" Elizabeth gasped. Her stomach felt like it had been dropped down an elevator shaft. *Gin-Yung sacrificed herself for him—for us.* It would have been so much easier if Gin-Yung had been selfish and unlikable. But Gin-Yung's goodness was tearing Elizabeth apart.

She looked up at Todd, her eyes watering. "It must be so horrible—I can't imagine what it's like for her."

Todd looked up at the blue sky. "I'm going back to the hospital tonight to bring her a few things. You don't mind, do you?"

"Why should I mind?" Elizabeth said with forced lightness. She clung to him to reassure herself that he was solid, afraid that he would slip through her fingers like grains of sand. But it was starting already. She could feel it.

Todd's eyes welled up, and his face reddened. *He knows it's happening too,* she realized. As he brought Elizabeth's hand to his lips and kissed the tips of her fingers, a warm teardrop fell from his lashes and onto her knuckle. "She needs company," he murmured, his voice breaking.

"Of course she does." The corners of Elizabeth's mouth trembled. She intertwined her fingers tightly in his, feeling his warm pulse.

Digging down deep, Elizabeth pulled up the words she was afraid she wouldn't have the courage to say. "She needs you, Todd."

"I know," he whispered, his breath soft against her cheek. "It's just that . . ." Todd trailed off and held her close, his body trembling. "I wish I could be two places at the same time, Liz."

Elizabeth bit the inside of her cheek to keep from bursting into tears. *But what about us?* she cried silently. She wanted to scream out loud and beat her fists against his chest and tell him how scared she was and cry shamelessly in his arms.

"Oh, Liz . . ." Todd choked back a sob, as if he read her thoughts. "Maybe this is a bad idea. I could go there tonight and tell her I can't visit her anymore . . . I'll say good-bye."

"Don't . . ." A stronger voice was coming from inside Elizabeth now, speaking beyond what her emotions would allow. Saying good-bye to Gin-Yung would break her heart, and they both knew it. She deserved better, as painful as it was for Elizabeth to recognize. "You go to her and take care of her, Todd. It's the right thing to do."

Todd cupped her face in his warm hands and stared into her blue-green eyes. "I love you more than I've ever loved anyone in my entire life." He took a deep breath. "You know that, don't you?"

Elizabeth nodded imperceptibly. "I love you too, Todd."

"Just because we're going to spend a little time apart doesn't mean we still can't love each other, right?" The rise in pitch of Todd's voice made Elizabeth wonder how sure he was of that.

"Right," she answered, tearing herself away from his gaze. A dark cloud of disappointment was hanging over her. Elizabeth had worked so hard to convince him to take care of Gin-Yung, and yet she was sad that he'd agreed to do so.

Todd brushed a golden strand of blond hair out of her eyes. "It's just temporary," he said. "It's not forever."

"No, it's not," Elizabeth agreed hesitantly. "It's just for a little while."

"You're so special to me, Liz." Todd tilted her face up toward his and kissed her tenderly on one cheek, then the other. His thumbs wiped away her tears. "When this is over, we'll be together again. I promise."

I want to believe you, but I don't know if I can, Elizabeth thought, trying to remind herself that what they were doing was the best thing possible for everyone.

Todd held up his hands and Elizabeth did the same, pressing hand to hand, palm to palm, finger to finger. Their eyes locked, chests rising and falling together. As Todd and Elizabeth's lips touched they breathed as one, their bodies melting together. She closed her eyes and savored the sweetness as their kisses deepened. Elizabeth wanted to remember the warmth of the heat rising up from Todd's face, the earthy scent of his skin, the brush of his rough cheek against hers, the beating of his heart, the taste of his lips. She wanted to make it the kiss of a lifetime—just in case it was to be their last.

SIGN UP FOR THE SWEET VALLEY HIGH® FAN CLUB!

Hey, girls! Get all the gossip on Sweet Valley High's® most popular teenagers when you join our fantastic Fan Club! As a member, you'll get all of this really cool stuff:

- Membership Card with your own personal Fan Club ID number
- A Sweet Valley High® Secret Treasure Box
- Sweet Valley High® Stationery
- Official Fan Club Pencil (for secret note writing!)
- Three Bookmarks
- A "Members Only" Door Hanger
- Two Skeins of J. & P. Coats® Embroidery Floss with flower barrette instruction leaflet
- Two editions of *The Oracle* newsletter
- Plus exclusive Sweet Valley High® product offers, special savings, contests, and much more!

Be the first to find out what Jessica & Elizabeth Wakefield are up to by joining the Sweet Valley High® Fan Club for the one-year membership fee of only $6.25 each for U.S. residents, $8.25 for Canadian residents (U.S. currency). Includes shipping & handling.

Send a check or money order (do not send cash) made payable to "Sweet Valley High® Fan Club" along with this form to:

SWEET VALLEY HIGH® FAN CLUB, BOX 3919-B, SCHAUMBURG, IL 60168-3919

NAME_____
(Please print clearly)

ADDRESS_____

CITY_____ STATE _____ ZIP_____
(Required)

AGE_____ BIRTHDAY_____ /_____ /_____

Offer good while supplies last. Allow 6-8 weeks after check clearance for delivery. Addresses without ZIP codes cannot be honored. Offer good in USA & Canada only. Void where prohibited by law.
©1993 by Francine Pascal   LCI-1383-193